IN LOVE WITH DECEIT

By Dorothy Brown-Newton

ACKNOWLEDGEMENTS

First and foremost, I want to give thanks to God. Without Him, none of this would be possible.

I want to say thank you to Raquel Williams and Leo Sullivan for making me a part of the family. I also want to say thank you to all of the readers that continue to support me. You guys rock.

A special thanks to my family that continue to support me and encourage me not to give up. Thanks to my daughter, Deriazsha Limbacker, and my friend, Linda Benjamin, who give me honest feedback when they proofread my books. Thanks to my sons, Rodger Jr., Jaden, and Jahzier, who give me time to write without complaining and to their father who holds them down when I'm sitting at the computer for hours. I love you guys.

CHAPTER ONE

CHINK

True, Jay, Liem, and Kev were posted up outside my house, leaning against Lah's brand new BMW, talking shit as usual. Liem's buster ass was out there flossing like that shit belonged to him, knowing good and well it belonged to his brother, Lah. Lah probably told his ass to take it to the car wash and bring it right back, but instead, his ass was out there trying to floss for that trick, Nailah. She would never give his broke pockets the time of day - unless she was asking him about Lah.

"Chink, how many times do I have to ask you to get your ass out of that window?" I heard my mom yelling from downstairs.

"Why do I have to get out of the window?" I yelled with a little more attitude than I intended to.

"Don't have me come up those stairs, Chink," she yelled back.

I never understood how she always knew when I was in the window. I swear I get so sick and tired of her treating me like I'm a fucking baby. Don't do this, don't do that. At seventeen years old, what the fuck can I do? I'm so sick of her acting like she's a warden, and I am her prisoner. I love my mom to death, but Rita Montgomery needs to detach the umbilical cord and let me breathe on my own. I picked up my phone to call my best friend, Polo, as I always did when I needed to vent. Her household was the opposite of mine. She had freedom, her mom even gave her a curfew, and she was allowed to date. Not my mom; she wanted my ass to go to school and be home right after. I'm praying that when I turn eighteen in a few months, she'll let up just a little because this shit is really becoming aggravating. I will be graduating high school next month with no plans on attending college - of course against my mother's plans for me.

The first thing out of Polo's mouth when she picked the phone up was a question she already knew the answer to. My mother was not letting me outside on a school night.

"Damn, Chink. You can never go anywhere. I hope she lets you come with me to Rasta's skating party on Saturday because that shit is going to be live," she said.

"Not unless your mom calls my mom and asks if I can spend the night over at your house. If not, you know she's not letting me go," I said, being honest.

"Chink, you're a prisoner in your own home," she laughed.

"It's not funny. This shit is really starting to blow my mind. She even called upstairs to tell me to get out of the window," I said, getting upset all over again.

"Who were you jocking that had your ass in the window anyway?" She laughed.

"Polo, who the hell still says jocking with your stupid ass?"

"How would you know what they say from the front porch because that's as far as your ass can go," she said, laughing.

"Whatever, trick. Just see if your mom can call and ask my mom tonight," I said before ending the call.

When I hung up the phone with Polo, I pulled out my book bag to get my assignment done that was due on Friday. 'My life as a prisoner should have been my title,' I thought to myself as I got started.

***

Polo's mom called my mom to ask if I could spend the night with Polo on Saturday, and my mom told her that she would let her know before Saturday. I knew she was going to make me wait it out because of my yelling back at her. I didn't care as long as her final answer was going to be yes.

I was standing at my locker at school minding my business, putting away my science book, because my classes were over for the day. I didn't have any science homework, so I didn't feel the need to carry that huge book home. After locking my locker, I turned around to find that Tally and Nisa, the school bullies, were standing behind me and getting all in my space. I grabbed my book bag and tried to go around them without causing an altercation with them. They were always trying to start trouble. There was no possible way for me to get by without bumping into one of them, so I did the polite thing.

"Excuse me," I said to Tally, who was standing closest to me.

"You're fucking excused," she said as she bumped me.

"Tally, why are you always trying to start a fight?" I said, getting irritated.

"I can do what the fuck I want, and if you don't like it, what the fuck are you going to do about it?" she asked, getting in my face.

POLO

I was standing at the end of the hall, watching Tally and Nisa fuck with my girl. I watched for a few seconds, just to see if Chink was going to do anything to stand up for herself. Of course she didn't, so I decided to come to her rescue once again.

"Is there a fucking problem over here?" I asked them.

Tally's big doofy ass looked like she saw the men in blue. Her scary ass backed up with her hands in the air. Nisa followed suit and began walking the opposite way.

"That's what the fuck I thought," I yelled at those two bitches, daring them to say something.

I was pissed right about now because I hated to see anyone pick with my best friend, and if we weren't on school grounds, I would have fucked both of those bitches up. They know that I don't play when it comes to my sis, so I don't understand why they keep coming for her, knowing I will get in their asses.

"Chink, you have to stand up to these bitches. That's why they fuck with you; they know you're not going to do shit," I said.

"Polo, I don't have time to be out here fighting for no reason."

"What do you mean for no reason? That bitch was straight disrespecting you," I said, getting heated.

"She can say what she wants as long as she doesn't touch me," she said, not knowing that I saw Tally bump her.

"If she touched you, what were you going to do?" I asked, taunting her.

"She didn't touch me, so there's nothing to talk about," she said, getting mad at me when she should have gotten mad with those two bitches.

Chink's mom has sheltered her for too damn long; she needs to learn how to stand up to these jealous bitches. That bitch straight bumped her ass, and she's talking about, "as long as she doesn't touch me." I know why they fuck with her; Chink is five feet seven, weighs one hundred forty pounds, and she has a nice little shape. What really has these bitches hating was her light brown complexion with her chinky, light brown eyes. That's how she got her nickname - because of those eyes of hers. She always has to deal with the hate from these bitches because they just can't stand all the attention she gets from just about every guy at the school.

Leaving school, Chink and I opted out of taking the bus. It was a nice day, so we decided to walk home. I could tell that Chink was a little nervous about being late getting home, but she didn't express it. I was telling Chink about my dude, Rick. I've been kicking it with him for a few weeks, and out of nowhere, she starts questioning me about Lah.

"Polo, how old do you think Lah is?" she asked with a serious face as if she hadn't just interrupted me.

"Bitch, I know you're not checking for Lah's ass?" I said, laughing.

"No, I was just asking you a question; you always have to take it somewhere else," she said, rolling her eyes.

"Yeah, okay, so is that why your ass was in the window last night?"

"Lah wasn't even out there. Stop playing. How old do you think he is?" she asked, copping an attitude.

"He's about twenty-two or twenty-three, which means he's too old for your hot ass. Ms. Rita's not having it anyway. You know your ass is not allowed to have a boyfriend," I laughed.

"I told you I was just asking, big head," she said, shaking her head.

"Yeah, okay. Oh, shit. Speak of the devil; there goes Lah right there."

11

Chink almost broke her neck trying to see Lah in the direction I was pointing in. I laughed so hard I had tears coming out of my eyes. That shit was too funny.

"I thought you weren't checking for him, liar?" I said, really laughing now.

"You play too damn much," she said, punching me in my arm.

"You should have seen your face when I said that shit. It was a mixture of lust and nervousness," I joked.

We joked about that shit all the way home, but her ass still didn't admit to feeling Lah though. We said our goodbyes when it was time for me to turn off on Francis Lewis Boulevard. She still had a few blocks to go because she lived over on 115th Avenue.

CHAPTER TWO

CHINK

When I walked into the house, it was quiet; Mom wasn't sitting in her favorite chair in front of the television. She always sat in that chair until I walked through the door. She always said that her brown chair with the plush cushion gave her a peace of mind. She would sit in that chair every day until I made it home safely. She was very overprotective; I always tried to tell her that she taught me well and that she didn't need to worry so much. I guess my being the only child made her feel like she had to worry. I remember when I was four years old. Mom was dropping me off to my first day of preschool, and she held onto my hand, tears falling, telling me all of the things to be aware of. The teacher assured her that I would be fine, and she reluctantly let go of my hand to let me enter the classroom as she continued to watch and observe. It became her daily routine for that first week to watch and observe from the hallway. Going into the second week, she began to trust that I would be fine, and gradually, she was comfortable enough to leave that hallway and go home. So you see, it started off very early on, and I love her for it, but I just wish she would let up just a little.

I ascended the stairs cautiously while mentally preparing myself for the tongue-lashing that was sure to come. Last time I was late coming home, Mom was so upset that she started hyperventilating. I was so scared after that day that I promised that I would never be late again, and I wasn't - until now. Mom's room door was open, but I didn't see her. I heard the water running from the bathroom in her bedroom, so I didn't attempt to enter.

"Mom, I'm home," I said nervously.

She didn't answer, so I figured that her not answering had to do with me being late getting home. I turned around to go to my room, but I felt a tugging that something wasn't right, so I went back in her room and knocked on the bathroom door. Receiving no answer, I turned the knob and pushed open the door, but something was blocking the door from opening. I started to panic as I muscled up the strength and pushed a little harder. Nothing could have prepared me for what was behind the bathroom door. My mom was on the floor, lying in a pool of her own blood. Her eyes were open as if she was looking right at me. I saw that she was holding the phone in her hand, which led me to believe that she was trying to call for help. I stood still for a few seconds, not knowing what to do, as the tears started to fall. The sight before me wasn't real. It couldn't be real.

I took the phone out of her hand, getting blood all over my hand, but I didn't care as I dialed 911.

"911. What's the location of your emergency?"

"117-11 115th Avenue."

"Is that between 115th Avenue and Francis Lewis Boulevard, ma'am?"

"Yes," I cried.

"What's your name and the number you're calling from?"

"Chink. I'm sorry; my name is Chasity Montgomery, and I'm calling from 718-322-9075."

Why the fuck do they always have to ask so many questions? Just send help already!

"Ma'am, are you still on the line?"

"Yes. Can you please just send someone to help my mom?"

"Ma'am, police and the ambulance are en route to help you. I need for you to stay on the line and try to answer a few more questions as calmly as you can. Tell me exactly what the nature of your emergency is."

"My mom is on the bathroom floor bleeding."

"Is the person conscious?"

"Is the person breathing?"

"I think she's dead," I said, crying.

"Is the person breathing, ma'am?"

"Are you safe?"

"Ma'am…"

"Ma'am, are you still on the line?"

"Ma'am, I know this is difficult, but I need you to calm down and talk to me."

"Ma'am…"

I dropped the phone as the tears poured from my eyes. Reality hit me as I recalled the words I'd spoken earlier about my mom possibly being dead. I got down on the bathroom floor, crying for my mother, and begging her to get up.

"Mom, please get up. Mom, please. I need you. Mom, wake up," I cried.

I tried to get her to wake up by shaking her, but she wouldn't get up. I didn't realize that the ambulance had arrived until I felt a hand on my shoulder and one under my arm, helping me up.

I was crying for my mom as they moved me out of the way so that they could get to her. I watched as they worked on her; they checked her vital signs, and I heard

16

one of the paramedics say that she had a weak pulse. It gave me hope; however, as soon as they began to lift her on the stretcher, she started going into cardiac arrest. I watched them give her CPR to no avail. I became hysterical as the paramedics were unable to bring her back. I really became inconsolable as I cried for my mom.

"Ma'am, is there anyone we can call for you?" he asked.

"Ma'am…"

I knew the officer was talking to me, but I didn't answer him. I wanted to say that I'm not a fucking ma'am and to leave me the fuck alone. I didn't want to call anyone; if they couldn't bring her back, there was nothing to talk about. All I wanted was my mom.

I heard my aunt's screams before she even made it to the room that I was in. She kept chanting, "I told you to leave."

My aunt told the officer that she was on the phone with my mom before she was attacked. She told them that the last thing my mom said before the phone went dead was, "He found me."

I was clueless as to what my Mom could have meant by "he found me." My family began pouring in; the officers wanted to question me, but my aunt told them that now wasn't a good time. My mom's body was still on the bathroom floor with a sheet now covering her. Being that she died in the home, she couldn't be moved until the coroner arrived. I went to my room because the scene was becoming too much to bear.

About an hour later, my aunt came to tell me that they took my mom. I continued sitting on the edge of the bed, weeping silently, and rocking back and forth. She insisted that I leave and come to her house because she felt it wasn't safe to stay here, but I told her that I wasn't leaving, and I didn't. She allowed me to stay after seeing I wasn't going to budge, but she had my uncle stay with me. I didn't mind because he left me to myself, and he stayed downstairs.

About an hour later, I found myself in my mother's bathroom, cleaning up her blood. The tears wouldn't stop. I heard the front door open and close downstairs, but I didn't even bother to stop to see who it was as I continued scrubbing the bathroom floor.

POLO

I walked into Ms. Rita's bathroom, and the sight before me broke my heart as I watched my best friend crying for her mom. I kneeled down in front of her.

"Chink, I just heard and rushed right over. I'm so sorry to hear about your mom," I said, trying not to cry.

"I just don't understand why this happened; maybe if I wasn't late, Mom would still be here," she cried.

"Chink, this isn't your fault, and had you been here, you probably would have gotten hurt too," I said, trying to stop her from blaming herself.

"I don't care, Polo! At least I would have been with my mom," she yelled at me.

I decided to just be quiet and be there for her as I grabbed a rag to help her clean up the blood off the bathroom floor and walls. After we were done with the bathroom, I helped Chink take a shower and get into some clean clothes. I really didn't understand what kind of monster would stab Ms. Rita up like that. She was a small petite woman who was always kind and would do anything for you if she could. I pray they catch the person responsible.

The next few days were hard for Chink as she just sat on her mom's bed, staring off into space. Her aunt sat with her during the day, and my mom allowed me to stay with her and her uncle some of the nights. The funeral was this Sunday coming; the family opted out of the traditional two-day service to have the wake and funeral on the same day. Her aunt felt that two days would have been too hard on the family. I honestly didn't know if Chink would bounce back from losing her mom because I know that I would be a basket case if I ever lost my mother. I promised to be there for her and to see her through this because that's what a real friend would do.

CHINK

After speaking to my aunt, I felt so bad that I had talked about my mom in a negative manner regarding her being overprotective and treating me like a child. I never knew that my mom was a victim of domestic violence by the father that I never knew. My aunt said he beat my mom constantly, and when she found out that she was pregnant, she attempted to run out of fear that he would hurt the baby. He found her a week later, and he beat her so badly that she was admitted in the hospital in the ICU. She remained there for a few months with doctors giving her a thirty percent chance of surviving, so no one knew at that time if she would make it or not. A month later, when the doctor gave my family the update that she and the baby were going to be okay, they moved her to Houston, Texas to stay with my Aunt Sherry until she was able to move into her own place.

My mom was doing well two years later when my father found her again. This time he snatched me, but not before beating her up very badly again. My aunt said that my mom was a wreck the whole time that I was missing, and she prayed that he wouldn't hurt me, knowing he was a dangerous man. Three weeks later, my mom's prayers were answered when she received the call that I was found somewhere in downtown Houston. For reasons unknown, I was left alone and unharmed. After that incident, my Aunt Sherry and her husband sent us to New York with my Aunt Shirley, who was my Aunt Sherry's twin. Aunt Shirley nursed my mom back to health and took care of me until my mom was able.

I had no idea that my mom endured so much pain, and now, fifteen years later, he found my mom and killed her. I cried until I had no tears left. What kind of man chases down a woman all these years later and stops at nothing until she's dead? I couldn't even imagine my mom doing anything that would cause anyone to hurt her the way he did.

Today we buried my mother. I would have to say that June 23rd will always be the worst day of my life because it is the day that I said goodbye to my mother. My aunts tried to be strong for me, and I really appreciated it because I knew they had to be feeling like they failed my mom. They saved their sister, only to lose her anyway to the sick man they'd helped her escape from. After it was all said and done, my only question to myself was where do I go from here? How do you go on living when the best part of you is gone? The police had no leads, not one fucking suspect in custody, and I was a little angry with my neighbors because most of them don't work, but nobody saw anything. I know that Ms. Ella from across the street stayed in her window, so she had to see something. I just prayed that the detective would catch a break in the case and find out who did this to my mom and put them under the jail. I didn't move out of the house in fear of losing my mom's presence. I could feel it in the home we'd lived in for as long as I could remember.

CHAPTER THREE

CHINK

(THREE YEARS LATER)

Today was one of the coldest days we've had this December. It was so cold that my lips felt numb. I rushed to get the groceries out of the trunk of my car and inside the house before I froze to death. "Damn," I yelled as a few of the cans from the bag fell out and began to roll down the sidewalk. I took the bags I was carrying and sat them in the foyer so that I could retrieve the other bags and get my cans of Goya pink beans that had rolled down the sidewalk. When I got to the top of the steps, my heart skipped a few beats as I saw Lah standing at the bottom of the steps, holding the remaining bags of my groceries.

"You scared the shit out of me," I said, holding my hand on my chest.

"I'm sorry; I wasn't trying to. I was sitting in my car when I saw your cans rolling away, so I stepped out to help," he said.

"Thank you," I said, grinning from ear-to-ear, not believing the man I'd been crushing on for years was standing on my porch.

"No problem. I'm just glad I was able to help," he said, smiling.

I held the door open and let him enter to take the rest of the groceries inside for me. I was so nervous that my once cold face was no longer cold. I felt my hands sweating; it was kind of funny to me that he still had that same effect on me as when I was a teenager.

"Why are you still standing at the door? Don't tell me you're nervous," he said.

"I'm not nervous; I was checking to see if my trunk was closed," I lied.

"As many times as you sat in that window just looking at me, you shouldn't be nervous," he laughed.

I felt my face burning from pure embarrassment. I only had one slat in the blinds lifted to peek at him, so how did he know I was in the window watching him?

"I didn't see you; I was told by someone very close to you," he said as if he knew exactly what I was thinking.

Now I was curious as to who told him, but I had an idea it was my sneaky ass friend, Polo.

"You're acting like I did this yesterday; it was a long time ago," I laughed.

"Yes, it was a long time ago, but it still doesn't change the fact that you did it." He laughed too.

"Did I deny it? No, I didn't," I said, answering my own question.

"Why were you always in the window watching me?" he asked.

Now he had me biting my nails, a terrible habit of mine when I became nervous. I ignored his question and began putting away my groceries. I looked over my shoulder, and I saw him bringing the rest of the bags to the kitchen, sitting them on the counter.

"It's okay, Chink. You don't have to answer my question. It's all good," he said.

He's so damn sexy, standing at six foot one, dark chocolate skin, low ceasar, full beard, straight white teeth, and don't let me get started on his thuggish stance. Just looking at him, he had my hormones all over the place. 'The way he says my name, he can definitely get it,' I thought as I watched him bring the last bag in.

"I'm going to leave you to your groceries, but before I go, I just want to say that I never got the chance to tell you how sorry I was, hearing about your mom. Ms. Rita was cool when she wasn't kicking us from sitting on her porch, chilling," he laughed.

"Thank you, and thanks for helping me with my groceries," I said quickly, trying not to tear up.

"Don't sweat it. You'll be seeing me again, and you can thank me with a home cooked meal since I saved your groceries," he laughed.

"Not a problem; I can hook you up with a meal, but it won't be any time soon because I'm doing it up for Christmas. I can guarantee you that I will not be doing no home cooked meals for a while after this big dinner," I said, seriously.

"Well, I guess I'm coming to Christmas dinner," he said as he walked out the door.

I let him out, and once the door closed, I stood in the living room doing the happy dance. I laughed as I walked back to the kitchen to finish up. I started singing Tamar's song, "Prettiest Girl," as I started putting my groceries away.

LAH

I sat in my car, watching her house, before pulling off. She didn't realize I could see her dancing through the picture window in her living room; she must have forgotten that the curtains weren't drawn. I couldn't help but smile because she was doing the happy dance because of me. Her girl, Polo, told me that Chink was feeling me, but I never got the chance to holla at shorty because shortly after, her mom passed.

I was on my way to check on my brother from another mother, Liem. He hit me up earlier, telling me he needed a few dollars. His mom did her best to raise him and his baby sister, but most days, ends just didn't meet. I helped out as much as I could; it was unfortunate he got the hand he was dealt. Our dad has been a deadbeat all our lives. I didn't understand how my mom, who's a psychologist at Mercy Hospital, got caught in his web of lies. My mom is smart and never let anyone get over on her; according to Liem's mom, my dad has always been a good-looking, smooth-talking nigga from the hood. I guess in her heyday, she was a fool for love because if a thug tried to holla at her now, he could forget it because she wasn't having it. You had to be making a certain amount of money, and be a part of the corporate world, for my mom to give you the time of day these days.

I feel for Liem and his mom, but at the same time, I'm happy that my mom and stepdad are well off. I wouldn't be able to live in the projects. I swear every time I go to Liem's crib in Baisley Houses, there's always piss in the elevator and lowlife niggas hanging around, doing nothing. I don't say that to say that I'm better than anyone else is or have anything against the ones who have no choice but to live there. I'm just saying that it could be a better living situation if they can get rid of the ones that tear down where they live, with no regards to the hardworking families that are trying to stay afloat.

My mom made sure I stayed in school and graduated. My current ride is the gift she got me after I got my associate's in computer programming. She wanted me to go back for my bachelor's, but I am done for right now. I work as a computer programmer at my mom's job, and I've been on the job for two years now. The job requires you to have your bachelor's, but my mom got me in. I will be going back to school, but for right now, I'm not ready. I'm making decent money and staying out the streets. I feel that's enough to keep her off my back for now.

Pulling up to the projects, the block was ghost; this was the first time that I didn't see anyone outside. I guess niggas are scared of a little cold weather; they must all be huddled up in the building. I hit Liem up and let him know I was downstairs. I usually go upstairs to say hello to his mom and sister, but I wasn't feeling riding in the piss filled elevator today because I was wearing a new pair of J's.

"What's up, Lah?" Liem said, getting into the car.

"Ain't shit. What's going on with you and the family?" I asked.

"Same story, different day. We're just trying to keep our heads above water," he said.

"Did you check out that info I gave you?" I asked him.

"Yeah, they're having open interviews on Thursday; I'm in there," he said seriously.

"I hope that shit works out. You working will eliminate some of the stress you're feeling," I told him.

"Well, I've got to get up. I'll hit you up later," I said, handing him an envelope.

"Good looking, bro. I appreciate it, and Mom appreciates it," he said.

"No problem; you know I've got you. Keep your head up, fam," I said, giving him a brotherly hug before pulling off.

I was going to make it an early night, but I decided against it as I headed to India's crib; she's a shorty I've been kicking it with. She was nothing serious, just my stress reliever for right now. I'm feeling shorty, but she has too many shortcomings; she's one of those shorties that wants shit handed to them but never wants to work for it. She has potential, but just like most females, she gets caught up with the mentality that her looks and body is all she needs to get what she wants, not knowing it's going to be her downfall.

I stay telling her that shit isn't going to fly with me. If she's not my girl, she will not reap the benefits that a girlfriend would. I thought she would take heed to what I was telling her because, like I said, I was feeling her, but she didn't. She came to the door wearing nothing but a t-shirt, with her ass hanging out, clearly showing that she didn't have any panties on, making a nigga want to fuck her right at the door.

"Why are you coming to the door with no clothes on?" I asked her.

"Don't act like you don't like seeing my ass hanging out," she said.

"I like seeing your ass hanging out. What I don't like is you letting the whole neighborhood seeing your ass hanging out," I said, getting irritated.

"Hold up; didn't you tell me last week that I'm not your girl, so stop acting like my man," she said, rolling her neck and shaking her hand in my face.

See, this is the reason she's not my girl; I try to teach her to respect herself, something her mama should have taught her a long time ago. Like I said, she's stuck on her big butt and a smile; she has yet to realize it takes a lot more to stimulate me. When fucking with her, it's just about getting off for me and killing time. I realize that you can't turn a trick into the woman your mom could love. I walked over to sit on the couch, and I swear, the stench of sex hit me dead in my face. Seeing the wet spot on the couch just confirmed what I was thinking.

"India, please tell me your ass didn't just get finished fucking on this couch," I said with my nose turned up from the smell.

"What the fuck are you talking about? My sister spilled juice on the couch a few minutes ago," she said with the stupid look on her face.

"Yeah, okay. Each time I try with you, I just get more disappointed. I'm starting to believe you will never be any more than a fucking nasty trick who doesn't even have enough respect to not fuck a nigga and think it's okay to tell the next nigga to come through."

"See, that's where you've got it fucked up. Like I told you earlier, you're not my man, and who I choose to fuck is my business."

I looked at this bitch as if she had two heads before walking out the door. She was right about two things. I wasn't her man, and she could fuck anyone that she wanted to; she just wouldn't be fucking me minutes after fucking dude. That nasty bitch probably told dude to roll out right after she read my text that I was coming through. Why do I always get caught up with these hoes?

I knew I should have taken my ass home like I started to. My work cell phone chirped, letting me know that I had a text message. I opened up the message that read: Deposit Completed.

I deleted the text, put my work phone back into my glove compartment, and continued to my destination with a huge smile on my face. That text was just what I needed to get me back in a better mood after witnessing that bullshit with India's ass.

CHAPTER FOUR

CHINK

Polo just got finished helping me put up the Christmas tree. Holidays were always hard for me, but I promised myself that I would be strong this year when I agreed to host Christmas dinner at my house. I started tearing up a little as I put the crystal ornament, that my mom got me for my first Christmas living at this home, on the tree. It was a gingerbread house with Chasity's Christmas embedded on front. I smiled in remembrance of all the good times we shared on holidays. I also hung all the paper ornaments I made her every year in grade school. Once the tree was completed, Polo and I decorated the staircase and hung the stockings on the fireplace.

I went back into the box of Christmas things to get the dressings for the windows and the front door. My mom never threw anything away; she always stored her things in the basement after taking them down every year. I just needed to pick up some new tablecloths because the one from the last year we spent with my mother caught fire. One of the candles fell and burned a big hole into it. I laughed at how I remembered that night so well. We all panicked when the tablecloth caught fire, but my mom remained calm as she put the small fire out.

Polo and I now sat at the table, sipping on some coconut Cîroc. I was telling her about my run in with Lah. We found out he is only two years older than me, which makes him twenty-two. He wasn't as old as we thought he was back in the day.

"So, did you get his number?" she asked.

"No, he just said he would see me again and that I owed him a home-cooked meal," I said, smiling.

"Sounds promising. He seems like a good dude, and you need someone in your life."

"He didn't say he wanted to date me, Polo," I said, laughing.

"He must want something. He could have sat his ass in that car and not helped, and those pink beans would be way across town right now," she said, continuing to laugh.

"You're stupid. I guess time will tell because if he wants to pursue something, he knows where I live," I said, not a bit convinced that he did want me.

Polo left around nine that evening, and I went upstairs to write in my journal. I have been doing this every day since my mom passed away; it was therapeutic to write as if I was having conversations with her. Sharing my life with her was easy because I know she's still here, watching over me. I even feel her presence sometimes; that's why I refuse to move.

I woke up feeling good after dreaming about Lah last night, something I haven't done since my teen years. I took a shower, got dressed, and was on my way. I had a few errands to run. My first stop was to Walgreens to get the candy my mom always bought for the Christmas holiday. Being this is the first year since her murder that I will be making dinner and inviting guests over, I'm going to make her proud and do it up as she did every year before her untimely death.

Christmas morning, I was up early cooking and baking. My Aunt Shirley was up helping and so was my Aunt Shelly, who was visiting from Texas. They agreed to help me get the food ready for our first big dinner without my mom. The last few years everyone celebrated among themselves with their immediate families. I always celebrated by visiting my mom's resting place, and this holiday will be no different. After the food is done, I will be making my visit while my aunts get the place ready for our family and friends to arrive.

Springfield Cemetery only stays open until four in the afternoon on Sundays and holidays. I wanted to leave soon because I still had to make a stop for my mom's flowers. The florist always closes on Christmas Day, so every year, I place an order for the bodega that sold flowers to have an arrangement made for this day. Polo offered to go, just as she did every year, but as always, I declined because my time with my mother was private and personal. I do allow her to visit with me on occasion because I know that she misses my mom just as much as I do.

LAH

I feel some kind of way about what I just did, but I had to remember that at the end of the day, it's a job. There is no room for emotions because emotions in this line of work could get you killed. I wasn't a contract killer; you can call me the hood killer. This wasn't a position I went looking for, it kind of fell into my lap.

One day, I was at the bodega picking up something to eat. The bodega was out of my way, but everyone knew that Smileys on the boulevard had the best sandwiches in the hood. Those joints had me drive way across town because a nigga would be feigning for them. As I was leaving Smileys, two dudes rolled up on me. One thing about me, I'm always on point. I peeped them grimy ass niggas from the door. I knew they were going to try me, and I was ready. I pulled out my 9mm and shot the first dude in his knee, dropping his ass. Then I quickly swung around and hit the second dude in his forehead with the butt of my gun until his ass went to sleep. I checked my surroundings again before hopping in my ride and pulling out.

I learned a valuable lesson that night; no matter how careful you think you are, there's always a possibility that someone is watching. I had to remember that when you do shit, you had to do it as if someone is watching, even if you don't see them.

Only positive thing about that situation was that the hood doesn't talk, and King Drone offered me a "lay a nigga down" per request job. He said that he liked how quickly I handled the situation and got ghost. He schooled me on always protecting my identity. King Drone said that I should have let them busters see that I was holding so that they could have backed off, and I could've caught them at another place and time. I'm just thankful that slip-up didn't cost me my freedom. Now older and wiser, I can do this shit with my eyes closed.

I made sure to stop by my brother Liem's crib, bearing gifts as I did every year. His mom always cooked a banging meal. I always admired his mom because no matter the situation, even falling on hard times, she always had a smile on her face. She made sure that her kids were good, even if that meant her going without. This would be the first year that I wouldn't be staying for dinner, though, because I had other plans.

"Lahmiek, you come here every year alone; you're such a nice young man. When are you going to meet a nice young lady to settle down with?" Mama D asked me.

"Mama D, I'm trying. These females today are all about playing games and only care about what you can do for them."

"That's so true. Those are the kind of girls Liem is into, and I'm trying to tell him that he needs a good wholesome woman, not these little girls," she said.

"Mom, I'm only twenty years old. A little fun never hurt anyone. I'm not ready to settle down," Liem defended.

"Liem, a little fun can hurt you. When you come home with your peter pan burning it's not going to feel like fun," she teased. However, at the same time, she was stating facts.

I was laughing so hard I had a coughing fit. Mama D had to come over to pat me on my back. That shit caught me off guard. Mama D is a trip, and that's why I loved her. She always kept it real with us.

"You're lucky Mama D is here because I was going to let you choke," Liem joked.

Once I caught my breath, I gave Liem dap, hugged Mama D, and kissed Cari on the forehead. I swear I love this family. His mom and sister weren't my blood family, but to me, they are definitely family.

"It's always a pleasure seeing you, Lahmiek. Be safe," Mama D said.

She's the only one I allow to call me by the name that my mom gave me.

"Same here, and call me if you need anything," I said.

"Boy, go on and get out of here. You already do so much for us already," she smiled.

"Family takes care of family, and all of you are my family," I said.

"Now you really better go before you have Mama D up in here crying," she said, wiping at her eyes.

I said my goodbyes again before leaving out the front door. I was a tad bit nervous as I pulled up in front of Chink's house. I wasn't nervous because I was visiting, I was nervous because I saw all of the cars and knew that she had a house full. I really didn't like being around people like that or having my picture taken, but by showing up, I wanted to prove to her that I was indeed interested in her. I was going to wait until her guests left, but once again, Polo put me on that Chink was having doubts that I wasn't feeling her as much as she was feeling me.

I checked myself in the rearview mirror. I know it's lame, but it is what it is. 'A nigga needs to be camera fly,'

I thought as I laughed to myself. I grabbed the gift bag out of the backseat before going to knock on the door.

CHAPTER FIVE

POLO

Steven was late picking me up, just as always. I should've been at Chink's house an hour ago. I wanted to be there to see the look on her face when Lah showed up. After I told him that she didn't think he was feeling her, he wanted to prove her wrong by showing up while all of her family and friends were over for Christmas dinner. Just as I was about to say fuck Steven and call a cab, he was blowing the horn. I was already pissed off, so I rolled my eyes as I got in the car and slammed the door, not caring that it was going to piss him off.

"You constantly bitching about me treating you like a child, but yet, you still act childish," he said.

"I'm not a child, and I'm not acting childish; you were supposed to be here an hour ago."

"So tell me, what's so hard about getting in the car and expressing that without the attitude and slamming my car door?"

"Being childish and being pissed off aren't one and the same, and you should learn the difference," I said, getting more aggravated.

"Patricia, I'm not about to sit here and argue with you. I was late because I had to stop by and at least say hello to my family that is visiting for the holidays," he had the nerves to say.

I hated when he felt the need to call me by the name I loved to hate, especially because he knows I hate to be called Patricia; he just did it to piss me off further. He's a grown-ass man who acts like a little bitch at times.

"So you stopped to say hello to family that I still have yet to meet, like you're ashamed of me or something."

"Look, how many times do I have to tell you that I can't just show up with you; I have to prepare them. Just be patient; I will tell them about you and then you can meet all of my family," he said.

His ass acts like a man that's never dated a younger woman before; I'm starting to think that he is full of shit, and this has nothing to do with my age and everything to do with the color of my skin. His being African American and my being white is why he doesn't want me to meet his family. I really don't understand what the problem is. I have lived in the hood my entire life, and not once has my skin color been a problem for anyone. For him to feel some kind of way about bringing me home is the quickest way to get his ass dumped because I refuse to be anyone's secret. And if color wasn't the issue, his ass must be hiding something else.

"Can we just go to your friend's house and have a good time without all the extra bullshit?"

I didn't ever respond; I just sat back, refusing to say anything else to his ass. His phone went off, alerting him that he had a text message. He was ignoring it, but when you ignore it, it continues to send an alert every few seconds. It was annoying the shit out of me.

"Are you going to answer the damn text? If not, can you at least stop the annoying alert from going off?" I said with much attitude.

He didn't say anything as I watched him read the text message; whatever it said, he wasn't happy, and his jaw tightened.

"Patricia, when I drop you off, I'm not going to be able to stay. Something came up," he said, offering no explanation.

I really could care less that he couldn't stay; I just wished that I went with my first thought and didn't even invite his ass. I'm getting sick of all of the disappearing acts and his broken promises. When he pulled up to Chink's house, I got out of the car with no words spoken, and I made sure to slam his car door just as hard as I did when I entered the car.

LIEM

I know that if Lah knew what I was doing, he would be disappointed. He's always told me that as long as I stayed in school and out of these streets, I wouldn't want for anything as long as he was breathing. It wasn't that I didn't believe him; I'm just starting to feel some kind of way about always having to have him take care of my family and me. Yes, he's my brother, but I should be taking care of my mother and sister; they are not his responsibility. The bus just stopped in Virginia, and that was about a thirty-minute stop. The driver left to gas up for the rest of the trip to North Carolina. I was meeting someone to make a drop in Virginia and North Carolina. This shit is easy money. The first dude I was meeting was supposed to meet me in the back of Bojangles'. I wasn't given a name; the only description that Drone gave me was that the dude would be wearing a brown scully hat, a brown parka, black jeans, and some brown Timbs. Drone said that they only went by a description of what the other would be was wearing because if anyone decided to snitch, they wouldn't have much to go on. It didn't make sense to me, but as I said, it was easy money, so I didn't question his logic.

I spotted dude as soon as I crossed the parking lot. That shit was quick and easy; no words exchanged. I rushed back to the bus area with enough time to grab a coffee to help keep my ass up for the rest of the ride. My mom has been calling non-stop because I left right after Lah left. I knew it was stupid to take a job on Christmas Day, but I needed the money. Rent was due in eight days. Mom didn't have it, but I was going to make sure that she got it - without me having to go to Lah. We reached Charlotte at about nine am. My last drop was at the gas station across the street from the Waffle House on Independence Blvd. I went to the Waffle House to have breakfast before retiring to my room at the Doubletree, where I was going to sleep until it was time to head back.

When it was all said and done, I was one happy motherfucker. I was able to pay my mom's rent for a few months. I was even able to take my little sis shopping for some school clothes because like me, she only owned maybe four pair of pants and a few shirts. I was even able to step my sneaker game up; a nigga was tired of wearing the same Jordan's that Lah got me a few months ago. I was hoping that Drone would need my services again because this shit here is easy money. My mom asked me where I got the money from to pay her rent for a few months and take Cari shopping. I hated to lie to her, but I couldn't tell her that I was drug trafficking to make some money to keep the family afloat, so I told her what I knew she would believe. I told her that Lah gave me the money. I just hoped that the next time she saw him, she wouldn't thank him for the money because then I would have some explaining to do. Lah wouldn't blow me up in front of my mom, but he would make sure I told him where the money came from.

I was now getting dressed because I was hanging with my boy, Tre, tonight at a club downtown to bring the New Year in. I wasn't really feeling hanging in the club tonight, but I didn't want to bring it in at home, sitting in front of the television, watching the ball drop as I did every year with Mom and Cari. Mom didn't really want me going out on New Year's Eve because every year you hear about shootings at the club. I assured her that I wasn't going to the club and that I was going to a get together at Tre's house to bring it in among friends. I wished her and Cari a Happy New Year's before heading out the door.

CHINK

I was in the mirror taking my wrap down; I was getting ready for Lah to pick me up. He invited me to his job's New Year's Eve party at the hospital. I didn't think he was feeling me, but when he showed up to my house on Christmas bearing gifts, I was elated. I couldn't even front as if I wasn't feeling him; that gesture alone had me walking around like a little schoolgirl with a crush.

We had a good time, and he enjoyed my family just as much as they enjoyed him. I was a little nervous about meeting his mom so soon, but he assured me that she would love me. It wasn't a girlfriend type meeting. It just so happens that she works at the hospital and will be in attendance, so he feels it's only right to introduce her to his date. I put on my stockings followed by the Christian Louboutins he got me for Christmas. I'm telling you that Polo is a trip; I know he went to her for my size. I have no idea why he would get me such an expensive gift. If he knew me, he would have known I couldn't care less about labels. Shit, I could have gotten fifty pairs of shoes from Payless with the money he spent on one pair of shoes. I really just wanted to throw on a pants suit because it was freezing outside. I decided against it though because I wanted to make a good impression on his mom in case we decided to take our relationship to another level in the future. My mom also taught me that a lady should always dress as such, especially when meeting the mom, so wearing pants wouldn't have been a good look.

If he was going to buy me some expensive shoes, he should have bought me a dress to match. The only dress in my closet that could probably look good with the shoes would be the black knee-length dress that I purchased from Macy's last month. It was designed to look formal with a casual edge. I loved the lace detailing. It was going to match perfectly with the lace on the Christian Louboutins. Don't get me wrong; I like nice things, but I also like what I like and that was shopping at my favorite stores like Forever 21, H&M, and Express.

The doorbell rang at exactly 7:30 pm. I grabbed my black trench dress coat and put it on, giving myself one last look in the mirror before opening the door. I couldn't help but stare at this fine man who looked so damn good. He grabbed my hand to help me down the stairs, and once we reached the last step, he faced me, taking all of me in. He was so close that I could smell the mint he was sucking on. I was tempted to bite my nails, but I used self-control.

"You're beautiful, and thanks for wearing the shoes." He smiled.

"Thanks for the compliment, and I love the shoes, but can we please have this conversation inside the car? I'm freezing." I smiled.

"My bad. You had me stuck for a minute, and I forgot how cold it was," he said.

I wasn't really cold because he had my body warm all over; I just said that I was cold because he was making me nervous. I felt like he was going to kiss me, so I chickened out and used that lame-ass excuse. Once in the car, he sat for a few minutes, staring at me intensely.

"What?" I said.

"Nothing. I'm just admiring how beautiful you are," he smiled.

"Thank you," I said, even more nervous now.

"Okay, I'm going to leave you alone and drive; I see I'm making you uncomfortable."

"No you're not," I lied.

He just gave me that knowing look as he pulled out of my driveway and headed toward our destination.

CHAPTER SIX
STEVEN

"So now you want to show up after I've been calling you, and you didn't have the decency to answer the fucking phone," India said as soon as she closed the door.

"How come every time I come here I've got to hear you bitching? You're never fucking happy. I'm here now, and you're still with the bullshit. I think you like hearing yourself bitch."

"You wouldn't have to hear me bitching if you pick up your phone once in a while. It could have been a fucking emergency, but do you care? No, because if you did, you would have fucking picked up your phone," India yelled.

"Well, it wasn't an emergency, so what's with all the attitude?" I asked.

"I'm tired of putting up with this bullshit; I'm tired of having to tell everyone that Tahira is my fucking little sister. You promised that we were going to be a family, but all you've done is kept us your fucking secret."

"India, I told you that shit is complicated, so miss me with the bullshit."

"So complicated that you couldn't come and see your fucking daughter on Christmas?"

"Okay, let's not pretend like you didn't know about my situation beforehand, so don't go acting brand new because you decided to have a baby like my situation was going to change."

"Well, how about we speed the process up and let your wife know that, not only do I have your first-born child, I'm pregnant with your second child," she yelled.

"Bitch, please. Let's not act as if you were seeing me exclusively. That baby could belong to anyone, and as far as you having my first-born, she's questionable as well, so let's not go there."

I thought that would shut her the fuck up. She's always running her mouth, trying to control shit; the quicker she realizes that she doesn't run shit, the better she will play her position. I dropped a few bills on the couch and bounced. I didn't even stick around to see the kid; I was out.

I called Polo, but she sent me straight to voicemail. I guess she's still upset, so I took my ass home to my wife.

"Hey, babe. How was your day?" I asked as I greeted my wife.

"It was good until the computer crashed at work. It was a mess for an entire hour; we had to log patients in manually on paper."

"Come here; let me give you a foot massage to try to release some of your stress."

"You know just what to say to make me feel better; I just hope the problem is rectified by morning," she said.

"I'm sure it will be, babe. Just lay back and relax," I said, massaging her feet.

I gave my wife a foot massage that put her to sleep like it always does. I carried her upstairs and put her in bed. I sat and watched her; my wife is so beautiful. Any man would do whatever it takes to have her and keep her, but for some reason, I can't stop chasing these young girls even though all I need is right here in front of me. I don't know what it is about younger women; they play games and most of them are possessive, but I just can't get enough of them.

I don't know if it's because I'm about to hit the big forty because I've always been attracted to them, but I never acted on it. This past year I have been creeping with Polo and India. I really got caught up with India when she had my daughter, Tahira; well, at least she claims she's my daughter. I was so happy that I was about to finally have my first-born, I blocked out all the signs that were in my face; she possibly wasn't mine. My wife of ten years, Karen, couldn't have children; we tried for years before seeking help. The tests came back, and my wife was told she had POI (Premature Ovarian insufficiency). We tried in vitro fertilization, but it didn't work, and she became depressed the first few years. The doctor suggested a support group, and that helped us a lot. She accepted the fact that she couldn't have children, but I still yearned for my own; so that's why when India said she was having my first-born, I continued a relationship with her, not caring to have the test done. I loved my wife, and India claiming to be pregnant by me again triggered something in me. If I have to hurt my wife, I want to at least know that the kids were definitely mine before confessing. I'm going to have tests done on both children if it's the last thing I do. I know that India is going to have a fit when I ask her to give me a DNA test for Tahira. I know that I have to wait until she has the baby before I can get a test for that one, but I just feel it's time for me to make things right with my wife.

KAREN

Steven had the nerve to bring his ass home as if shit was sweet between us; he just doesn't know how much he makes my skin crawl. When he touched my feet, I pretended to fall asleep like I always did. He thinks I don't know about all the other women, but I have known for years. I have been trying to have a child with Steven for many years to fill the void of having my child snatched from me when I was only fifteen years old. It happened many years ago, but it still feels like yesterday to me. I was in high school when I met my first love, Troy. We were inseparable, and we did everything together. On our one year anniversary, Troy took me out to eat and to the movies; we went to see Love & Basketball. I swear after seeing the movie, I wanted to be just like Monica and Q. I decided to give my virginity to Troy that night because at the time, I just knew that we were in love. I was sure that we were going to get married and live happily ever after, but boy, was I wrong about the living happily ever after part.

When I found out I was pregnant, my mom kicked me out of the house; she told me that since I was grown enough to lay down and get pregnant, I needed to take my grown ass and let that man take care of me. I didn't care

57

that she kicked me out because I just knew that Troy wouldn't have a problem taking me in. I packed a suitcase, grabbed the few dollars that I had, and used the house phone to call a cab to Troy's house. I didn't call ahead like I usually did because my mom took my cell phone that she had bought me, and after she saw me using the house phone to call my cab, she told me not to touch her phone again. She was upset and just trying to get a reaction out of me by taking the phone and telling me that I couldn't use the house phone. She still didn't get one out of me because I knew that Troy would get me a new phone without a doubt. I was having his baby, so I knew for sure that he wasn't going to let me go without having one. The cab ride was fourteen dollars, leaving me with six dollars to my name. I grabbed my suitcase from the trunk of the cab and marched up to the front door. I was so excited to finally be able to spend the rest of my days waking up next to the love of my life. I knocked on the door with a big smile on my face; I couldn't wait for him to answer the door. My smile faded when I saw his mom answer the door with tears in her eyes.

I sat my bag down on the porch and asked Ms. Rita what was wrong, and she cried out that they killed her baby. It took me a minute to realize that she was telling me that my first everything was gone. It seemed that Troy was into some things that I wasn't aware of; I had no idea that all the times he told me he was going out of town to visit his dad upstate, he was actually drug trafficking.

According to his best friend, Ronnie, they were set up. Ronnie said two men pulled out on them, demanding the bag. Ronnie said they both ran, but he got away. He said that they chased Troy because he had the bag, and when they caught up to him, they shot and killed him. Did I believe his story? No, I didn't, and to this day, I still don't. Long story short, his mom took me in. She told me that I could stay with her, and we would raise Troy's baby together, because that's what he would have wanted. I had nowhere else to go, so I agreed. I remember going into labor at only eight months pregnant. I kept telling Ms. Rita that I needed to go to the hospital, but she just kept telling me to relax, and she gave me something to drink. She said it would help with the contractions, and when the contractions were at five minutes apart, we would go to the hospital. All I remember about that night was waking up, left for dead, and my baby was gone. I cried day in and day out for my baby girl. I was going to name her Isis Montgomery because Troy always said that if he ever had a baby girl, he would name her Isis, and his son would be a junior. I never got the chance to honor his request, but someday, I will be bringing his baby girl home where she belongs.

The next day at work I knew I needed to concentrate on the matter at hand and that was to find Lahmiek. I saw him sitting at his workstation, looking over some paperwork. I walked over, not really knowing what I was going to say as I approached him.

"Good morning, Lahmiek. I'm sorry to bother you, but I wanted to know if you can take a look at my computer."

"Good morning, Karen. What seems to be the problem? And did you put a work order in?" he asked.

"The screen keeps going in and out, and no, I didn't put a work order in. I didn't know that I needed to."

"Well, I don't have a problem checking it out, but I'm going to need you to put a work order in. I will need the work order number that they give you because I will need to use it if your computer requires me to order a part to fix it," he said.

"Not a problem; so when I get the work order, do I bring it to you?" I asked.

"No, once you get the work order, I will see it on my work log for the day and come to your workstation. If you call it in now, I should be to your workstation within thirty minutes," he said.

"Okay, thank you for your time. See you in a few," I said, smiling.

Damn, I should have known I needed a work order. Now I have to continue to log in my patients manually for at least thirty minutes because of my little white lie. When he gets to my workstation, I have to work on getting him to open up because I need some information from him.

Just as he said he would, Lahmiek came to my workstation exactly thirty minutes later. I had to think quickly about how I was going to start up a conversation before he realizes that the only thing that was wrong with my computer was that the plug had been pulled out from the back of the computer.

"Hello again, Lahmiek, and thank you for coming back so soon. Being that the system was out yesterday, I'm really behind and need to get caught up," I said, not knowing what else to say.

"Not a problem. I should be done fixing your computer in no time," he said.

"How did you like the New Year's Eve company party?" I asked him.

"I had a good time; I was a bit nervous because it was my date's first time meeting my mother."

"I saw you guys in passing; she's beautiful and seemed to be down to earth. I'm sure your mother loved her," I said.

"She didn't really get to have a conversation with her because my mother was busy doing her hosting thing, but we had a good time."

"I'm sure she will have plenty of opportunities to meet your mother on a not-so busy occasion. I could tell that you really liked the young lady," I said.

"We haven't known each other long, so I haven't initiated another meeting yet because I don't want to make her feel like I'm rushing her into something. I thought by bringing her to the party, my mom could at least feel her out and let me know what she thought of her, but like I said, she never got the time to do it," he said.

"I'm pretty good at that type of thing; if you need me to feel her out for you, let me know," I said, hoping he didn't think I was strange for offering.

"I'll let you know, and thanks. Your computer is all set to go; the adapter wasn't plugged into the wall," he said.

"Silly me. I'm sorry for wasting your time," I said, hoping he didn't see right through me.

"Not a problem. Enjoy the rest of your day," he said, walking away.

CHAPTER SEVEN

LAH

I don't know what my co-worker, Karen, was trying to pull by pretending something was wrong with her computer. I know for a fact that she pulled out the adapter, but I didn't know what her game was. I hope she's not trying to get at me because she's old enough to be my mother. Don't get me wrong, she looks damn good for her age and her body is on point, but I couldn't go there if I wanted to. For some strange reason, looking at her with the same eyes that my girl has would be a constant reminder of Chink. Just the thought of her made me smile; I really had a good time with her at the party, and I am looking forward to seeing her again.

India had the nerve to hit me up, talking about she's pregnant. I asked the bitch by whom, and she had the nerve to cop an attitude. I know that she's out there, and I wasn't the only person that she let hit. I strapped up every time I ran up in her; my mama didn't raise no fool. I told her to hit me up when it was time to take that DNA test, but she caught an attitude and ended the call with the quickness. I didn't have time for India's ass trying to mess up what I have going on with Chink with some "you're my baby's daddy" bullshit. On my way out, I saw Karen standing at the elevator; I was about to go in the other direction, but she saw me.

"Hey, Lahmiek. I see it's that time for you too."

"Yeah, I'm headed home. Did the computer give you any other problems today?" I asked her.

"No, it didn't, and you saved my patients from having to wait long. Thank you again because it probably would've taken me all day just to figure out the adapter wasn't plugged in," she said, not looking like she believed the words that were coming out of her own mouth.

"You're quite welcome again," I said, ready to part ways.

The elevator finally came, and we both exited on the parking lot level and said goodnight. I had to get away from her because I didn't want to give her any ideas that I was interested in her. I sent Chink a text to let her know that after I went home to change my clothes, I would be on my way. I haven't spoken to my brother since Christmas; I need to get up with him and make sure that he and the fam are good. I got to Chink's place about an hour later with dinner and a movie because when she texted me back, she said she had a hard day at work today.

I told her she didn't have to cook anything because I would pick up dinner and a movie.

Chink opened the door, wearing a messy bun in her hair, a tee shirt, and sweats, and I tell you no lie, she was still beautiful. I kissed her on the cheek before entering the house. I sat the food on the table. I had picked up a takeout order from Outback; I got Chink the grilled salmon with mixed vegetables, and I got myself the grilled Mahi with mixed vegetables. I grabbed us both a slice of carrot cake with coconut-filled icing for dessert. I have been feigning for carrot cake since Christmas Day when I tasted the one her aunt made. I knew it wouldn't taste as good as hers would, but Outback would have to do for now until she made it again. I washed my hands and set the table while she put the food on the plates. I wanted to get a bottle of Hennessy, but I didn't want her to think I was trying to get her drunk.

"So, do you want to tell me about your hard day at work today?" I asked her in between bites.

"It's just that sometimes I don't understand why some of my clients think I'm a miracle worker. Sometimes I have to work with next to nothing, because some of their hair is about a few inches long, but they still get upset when braids don't hold," she said, and I laughed.

"I don't mean to laugh, but women are hilarious; they know they didn't have any hair when they left home, so if there's anything the hair dresser can do for them, they should at least be appreciative."

"My point exactly. The client that I'm speaking of came into the shop, and she had a bald spot in the front of her hair. I told her that she didn't have enough hair in the front to use to cover the bald spot once I put the weave in because it was just that wide. I suggested that she get a stocking cap weave, or I could box braid the front and have the braids cover the bald spot and weave the back."

"What did she say?" I asked.

"She was like, 'Did I ask for fucking braids? If I wanted braids, that's what I would have asked for when I first walked in.' Had I not tried to work with her and suggest what could be done to help with her situation, I probably would have let it slide, but I lost it and sent her ass out of my chair and out of my salon. Even the other beauticians were trying to tell her that it would work and look very nice, but she shunned them too," she said, getting upset all over again.

"Calm down, tiger," I joked, and she laughed.

"I'm telling you, I'm not that person, and Polo calls me a punk all the time, but if you take me there, I can quickly become that person," she smiled.

We spent the rest of dinner talking about our jobs. I told her that I believed an older co-worker was trying to come on to me today, and she laughed. I told her not to laugh because she could have definitely gotten it. I also told her that Karen favored her a little bit - just an older version. Her reply was, "She may look like me, but trust, there is only one me." I had to agree with her on that.

Dessert was good, but just as I expected, it wasn't as good as her Aunt Shelly's. Too bad she lived in Texas. Chink said that if I played my cards right, she would have her aunt send me a couple of pies. I plan on playing my cards right.

"So, what movie did you get?" she asked.

"My boy, Kevin Hart's, *Let Me Explain*," I said.

"Good, because I need a good laugh after the day I had," she said.

I enjoyed watching Chink laughing and enjoying herself, forgetting about her day at work. She had the cutest laugh, and without giving it much thought, I pulled her into my arms and we sat there, laughing together and enjoying each other's company. Kevin Hart is a funny dude; I laughed so much that my stomach hurt, and Chink laughed so hard that tears were coming out of her eyes. I had a good time tonight, but all good things must come to an end. We both had to work in the morning, so she walked me to the door. I kissed her on her lips, and that led to us making love with our tongues. I broke the kiss because if I didn't, I wouldn't have been able to control what happened next. I hugged her goodbye, kissed her one last time on the lips, and left.

I forced myself to have self-control tonight because I want more with Chink than some quick fuck. I wanted to make sure that when we decided to sleep together, it would be special. I didn't want us to just have sex, knowing I have to leave because of work the next morning. I wanted to be able to cuddle with her after and go for round two in the shower the next morning.

LIEM

Lah just left my house; he stopped by because he hadn't heard from me in a while. He asked me if I'd found a job, and when I said I hadn't, he started to give me the side eye. He then gave me the, "I hope you're not out in these streets" speech. I told him that I wasn't and that I was doing side jobs in the neighborhood. Standing there, rocking the newest J's, a pair of Topman ripped jeans, and a Black Pyramid track jacket, he had to know that I was lying, but he didn't voice it.

I've gone on a run since Christmas day and was about to make another one; this shit was too easy. I was on my way to Nailah's crib; she finally decided to give a nigga some play. I looked around before hopping in my rental because if Lah saw me in this rental, he would have definitely known what was up. I'm sure he knew, but he let the conversation go; I knew he was going to pick it back up at a later time. I was only going to be able to kick it with her until about nine tonight because my bus was leaving tonight at ten. I pulled up to Sutter Gardens Projects, and she was standing outside waiting because she said that she didn't want me to wake up her grandmother by ringing the buzzer. I knew there had to be more to it because it was only seven in the evening.

"You didn't have to stand in the cold to wait for me. I could have called you when I was outside," I said when she got in the car.

"It's okay; it's not that cold out," she said, lying. It was obvious that she was freezing.

"So what do you want to do?" I asked her.

"Well, we really can't do much, being you said you can only hang out until nine, so I'm good with just getting something to eat," she said.

"So, let's go to the Olive Garden. Is that cool?" I asked.

"Nah, let's go to Applebee's. Olive Garden don't have shit I want," she said.

"Applebee's it is then."

"If you don't mind me asking, what did you do to get money because you came up like overnight?" She laughed, but I didn't.

"I don't mind you asking, but answering is where I mind," I said.

She rolled her eyes as if she had an attitude, but I didn't care. My thing was why can't we just go out and have a good time? How does my money and how I make it even fit into the conversation? I know she's a gold digger and only agreed to hang out with me because she

71

saw dollar signs; but damn, she could have been a little discreet with it. We got to the restaurant, and she ordered drink after drink. She was on her third drink, and the food hadn't even arrived yet. The more she downed her drinks, the more she felt comfortable with putting her gold digging ways on Front Street.

"So Liem, do you think you can get my hair and nails done?" she asked, rubbing my hand from across the table.

I started to go in on her, but I've been chasing her for years. Now was my chance, so I played it cool.

"And what are you going to do for me?" I asked.

"We can go the telly, but don't you have to be somewhere by ten?" she asked.

"Yeah I do, but if we skip dinner, we can pull it off," I said, fucking with her.

"Nigga, you done lost ya mind. I'm not fucking on no empty stomach," she said a little too loud, getting unwarranted attention.

"Okay, Nailah, bring it down. You don't have to let everyone know what we're talking about," I said, somewhat embarrassed by her outburst.

"Well I guess you have to take a rain check," she said.

"I guess," I said, saying no more as the server placed our food on the table.

72

I had nothing else to say; I just wanted her to eat so that I could drop her ass back at home. Then I could park the car somewhere near Chrystie Street where I would avoid a ticket until I got back. I'd rented the car for two weeks, so I was good on not returning it while I was gone. After dinner, it was time to drop Nailah's ass off. When we got to her building, she got out of the car and made sure to slam the car door as hard as she could because I didn't give her any money. As I said, I knew she was nothing more than a trick, but I was hoping that she would actually try to get to know me before she went for the kill. Had she done that, she would have seen that I was a good dude, but she didn't even take the chance. All she saw was dollar signs. I wasn't an ugly dude, so I knew that I didn't have to pay for pussy; it's just that I was really feeling her, always have, ever since high school. I just wanted to take her out, hoping that she would see past the dollar signs and actually try to get to know me.

CHAPTER EIGHT

KAREN

After talking to Lahmiek just about every day, I learned that Chink owned a hair salon called Chasity's on Merrick Blvd. I just pulled up to the salon and sat in the car for a few minutes to get my thoughts together. I got out of the car and walked into the salon, looking for her.

"Hello, ma'am. How can I help you?" the receptionist asked.

"Yes, I was referred by a close friend, and I wanted to get a wash and set today," I said.

"Do you have an appointment or is this a walk-in? If you're walking in, I have to let you know that we are very busy today," she said.

"No, my friend didn't tell me that I needed to make an appointment. How long is the wait for a walk-in?" I asked, not really wanting to wait too long.

"It will be at least an hour's wait because, like I said, we are very busy today. Do you have anyone in mind to do your hair since you were referred?"

"No, I'm fine with the next available stylist."

I started to make an appointment for another day, but when I saw Chink moving about, I decided to wait. I sat and just watched her as she worked. I tried my best to stay seated and not get emotional, but this is the closest I've been to her since she was snatched from me. She had my eyes, but everything else was all Troy. While I waited, my mind took me back to the day I finally decided to approach Rita.

I sat in my car on that cold, brisk morning, waiting for Chink to leave for school so that I could speak with her grandmother. Yes, her grandmother. I had the heat on full blast, but I was still cold and having chills. I think I wasn't feeling the heat because I couldn't focus on getting warm; my focus was on trying to figure out how I was going to approach the situation. I watched as the front door opened, and Chink walked out, wearing a cute lavender hat with a white ball on top. Her bangs were hanging out of the front of the hat, and she looked cute with her matching lavender North Face jacket. Rita stayed on the porch, watching her until she turned the corner, and she was no longer able to see her. When Rita closed the door, I got out of my car and rang the doorbell. When she answered the door, I could tell she didn't recognize me.

"How can I help you, ma'am?" she asked.

"Ms. Rita, it's me, Karen, Troy's girlfriend," I said. I had that same feeling I had when I showed up at her door all those years ago.

"Oh my Lord, Karen," she gasped.

"Ms. Rita, I'm not here for trouble. I just need to speak with you," I said

I watched her as she contemplated whether she was going to let me in or not. I must say that she aged well; she didn't look a day over forty. To think, I used to look up to this woman. She loved her son and told me she loved me as if I was her own daughter, just to leave me for dead. I felt myself getting angry, and I tried to warm my facial expression because I didn't want it to deter her from letting me in. After a few minutes, she opened the screen door and allowed me to enter. I walked into the living room and took a seat; she sat down across from me. She was wearing a sympathetic expression, but I didn't need her to sympathize with me. I needed answers. The bitch didn't feel sorry when she snatched my fucking baby and left me to die.

"Ms. Rita, I'm not here to sugarcoat anything. I need to know why you took my child and left me for dead."

"Karen, I had so much going on at the time. Before Troy was born, I had a little girl named Symone; she was two years old when she died. I left her outside unattended to run inside to answer the telephone, and when I returned, she was floating in the pool. I jumped in, pulled her out, and started CPR, but she was already gone," she cried.

"So if you know what it feels like to lose a child, how could you snatch mine?"

"After losing Symone and then Troy, my mental state just wasn't the same. When Symone's father, Drone, left me, I was a mess. A few years later, I met Troy's father, and when I told him that I was pregnant, he left me too. Troy was all I had; when I lost him and found out that I could have a part of him again… that's what caused my actions. When Chink was six months old, I ran into Symone's dad, and we got back together, but he became very abusive. He still blamed me for her death, so not only was I running from him her whole life, I was running from you and the authorities too. I couldn't have another baby snatched from me," she said, continuing to cry.

"But she wasn't your baby, she was mine!" I shouted, getting emotional. "I lost the love of my life, my first everything, and you snatched the only part of him that I had left. Yes, he was your son, but the child he and I created out of love belonged to us, not you. You had no right," I said as the tears fell.

"Karen, I apologize. I wanted to bring her back so many times, but I was in fear for my life and for Chink's life. The man that she thought was her dad beat me every chance he got; he even snatched her one time, and I thought I would never see her again. When God sent her back to me, I couldn't give her back. You should be thankful that I kept her safe," she said. Ms. Rita was no longer crying and was becoming angry.

'The nerve of her!' I thought to myself. If she hadn't snatched my child, she would have had no reason to protect her. 'I'm supposed to be thankful that you kidnapped my child?' I thought as the rage began to build up in me. She was trying to justify her actions for a situation that she not only put herself in but included my child in as well - a child that didn't belong to her in the first place. She thinks that because they made it out safely, it's all good. She's got life fucked up if she thinks that she gets off the hook because she escaped her crazy boyfriend. I missed out on raising my daughter as my own, a daughter that thinks her grandmother is her birth mother. She didn't give me a chance to know my child and tell her about the father that she never got to meet; she took that away from me.

"Ms. Rita, this is how this is going to go. I want to meet my daughter; it's been seventeen years, and I refuse to go another day without my daughter knowing who her mother is."

"Karen, I understand how you're feeling, but she's already an adult. Why can't you just let us be?"

"Because she's my child, and not one day went by that I didn't think of her. Besides, she has the right to know who her mom is and who her dad was."

"Karen, please, I'm begging you not to do this. Do you know what this will do to her?"

"Ms. Rita, I'm going to go now, but I will be back this evening. If you haven't told her by then, I will, and don't think about running again because I have someone watching the house," I lied as I got up to leave.

When I got back to her house that evening, I saw the yellow tape and police cars. The street was blocked off, so I parked, walked up the block, and asked one of her neighbors what happened. She said that someone murdered Ms. Rita, and the tears fell. I wasn't crying for her, but because I was back at square one. I could have approached Chink, but how could I approach her while she was mourning for the woman who she believed to be her mother. Now, three years later, I'm sitting inches away from my only child. I didn't even know that I was crying until the receptionist asked me if I was okay, bringing me back to the present. I got up to leave because my emotions were all over the place. But I made a promise to myself that I wasn't going to wait any longer; I will be approaching Chink to let her know that I'm her mother, and I hope she gives me a chance to explain and prove it to her.

POLO

"Hey, girlie. I haven't heard from you in a while," I said when Chink picked up her phone.

"I'm sorry, girl. Between work and spending time with Lah, I forgot about my girl, but you forgot about me too," she said.

"Girl, college is kicking my butt. Between that and dodging Steven's ass, who didn't get the memo to leave me the hell alone, it's killing me."

"I didn't get the memo either. What happened?"

"I just got tired of his many excuses as to why I haven't met any of his family or friends; it just seems suspect to me, so I'm pulling myself from the equation before I get hurt."

"I feel you. His ass either has a girlfriend, or he's married."

"My point exactly. Anyway, how are things going with you and Lah?"

"It's going better than I expected. Girl, he laid a kiss on ya girl that had my ass wanting to fuck him at my front door."

"Don't tell me you haven't given him any yet."

"It's not like I haven't been ready to give his fine ass my virginity, but he's been nothing short of a gentleman."

"Shit, if he hasn't jumped your bones yet, he must really be feeling you, girl."

"I hope so; I still haven't given him the test yet."

"Girl, you better not make that man sit through The Seat Filler. Any man that can pass that test isn't the man for me," I laughed.

"Well, he will be the man for me. Any man that sits through a chick flick and doesn't complain is my kind of man," she said.

"Yeah, okay. Lah better tell your ass hell to the fucking no."

"He won't. Anyway, I have to get back to work, and I will speak to you later."

"Okay, girl. I need to stop by the library anyway before I leave this damn school."

After I got off the phone with Chink, I went to the school's library to pick up a book for my criminology class. I was tired by the time I left the library; I just wanted to go home, take a shower, and call it a night. I didn't have to be back to work at Duane Reed until tomorrow evening. It wasn't my dream job, but it's a means to an end until I finish school. As soon as I walked out of the school, I saw Steven's ass leaning against his car, waiting for me, and my whole attitude shifted. I was not in the mood to deal with his foolishness as tired as I was.

"Steven, what are you doing here? I told you it's over; I can't do this with you anymore. I deserve better."

"And I'm trying to give you better, but you keep pushing a nigga away," he had the nerve to say.

"Steven, I'm twenty years old, and you're twenty years my senior; so with that being said, it was destined to fail, and you didn't help the relationship by acting as if you didn't care about me or my feelings."

"Come on, you know that age is just a number, and I care for you more than you know."

"Steven, I can't tell; I've asked you and continued to ask you to let me meet your family and still nothing."

"That's because it's complicated, and I really don't see what's so important about you meeting my peoples. This is about me and you."

"Listen, I had a hard day today, and I'm tired. I just want to go home; I will call you later."

"Well, at least let me take you home."

"No need. I have my mother's car. I will call you tonight," I lied as I walked off.

Steven's a grown fucking man; yet, he's still playing kiddie games. I may be young, but I'm not for the games, and if he doesn't know, eventually he will figure it out and go bark up somebody else's tree. I didn't have my mom's car, and I was hoping his ass wasn't on some stalkerish shit. I silently prayed he didn't follow my ass to the bus stop. When I got to the bus stop, I bent down to put my pants inside of my boots because the cold air was going up my legs. As soon as I bent down, I heard a car horn trying to get my attention. I was ready to go ham on his stalking ass, but it wasn't Steven. It was Liem.

"Hey, Liem. What's up?" I said, happy that it wasn't Steven.

"I'm headed your way. Do you want a ride?" he asked.

"Hell yeah. Shit, it's freezing out here," I said, getting into the car.

"How have you been? I haven't seen you since high school," he asked.

"I've been good. Just busy as hell doing this college thing."

"You go to John Jay College?"

"Yeah, and it's kicking my ass."

"Damn. What made you choose Criminal Justice?"

"I always wanted to work either doing forensics or in the nursing field."

"Good luck with that. After high school I didn't want to see another classroom," he laughed

"You sound just like Chink, but I'm doing this college thing now so that I can do bigger things later."

"I feel you. How's Chink doing? I know she's with my brother, but he hasn't brought her around yet."

"She good. I hardly get to see or talk to her; she's all wrapped up in your brother."

"I haven't spoken to him much lately either. Well, I'm glad he found someone. My mom has been telling him to find someone to settle down with for the longest."

"So, what's up with you, Liem? What you got going on?" I asked him, giving him the side eye.

"I'm not going to lie; I'm out here doing me, but it's a temporary gig."

"Not trying to be all up in your business, but it's never a temporary gig. Most get addicted to the fast money, cars, and the lifestyle that comes with it and get stuck."

"I can't argue with that because I constantly say it's going to be my last time, but I'm still out here."

"Well, if you're going to be out here, just be careful."

"My ass fronting. I'm not in these streets, just a little drop here and there," he said, smiling.

85

"Still be careful. Shit can go wrong with just a drop here and there too," I smiled.

We talked the rest of the ride to my house. I couldn't wait to tell Chink that he's kind of cool, not so much the wanna be that we thought he was. He's in the wrong business for me to give him play, but he seemed to be just as charming as his brother, Lah.

"Why did you get so quiet all of a sudden?" he asked.

"No reason," I answered.

"I'm sorry if I was boring you, Ms. Thang," he laughed.

"You're such a character and far from boring."

"So, do you want to stop for a bite to eat before you head home?"

"I had a hard day at school. I'm beat; I just want to go home to shower and go to bed."

"So you're not going to eat tonight? C'mon, you can't be that tired," he asked, giving me the sad face before he burst out laughing.

I thought about it, and I was a bit hungry, so I agreed to go with him to get something to eat. I couldn't stop laughing when he pulled up to the drive thru at McDonald's.

"What you don't like McDonald's?" he laughed.

"Hell yeah, I love McDonald's. I just thought that we were going to a restaurant," I said, still laughing.

"You said that you were tired, so I figured I would just get you something to go."

"That was thoughtful of you. Get me a number one with a sweet tea."

"Cool, what about apple pies?"

"Nah, I'm good on the sweets. The tea is enough."

He ordered my food, but he didn't get anything for himself.

"You're not going to order something for yourself?" I asked him.

"After I drop you off, I'll grab something to take home for myself and the family."

"Oh okay. How are they doing?" I said, putting a couple of fries in my mouth.

"They're good, and how is your mom doing?"

"She's doing okay. I hardly get to see her much; her work hours are crazy."

"So she's always working like my mom, huh?"

"Yep, that's why I'm putting this work in, even though college is kicking my butt. I want better. Not only for myself, but so my mom doesn't have to work so hard."

"I feel you. A lot of people won't understand why I do what I do, but I swear it's to help my mom with the bills. I mean I flossed a little on myself, but it comes with the territory."

"Well, if that's why you started, you should be good now. You should have a little nest egg to hold you down until you find work."

"I got one more run to make this week and then I'm out. That's my word. So how about next weekend you let me take you to get a real meal?"

"If you're true to your word and leave this game alone, you can take me out to enjoy a real meal. But don't do it for me, do it for your freedom," I said seriously.

He gave me the head nod, followed by him saying that he could show me better than he could tell me. We left it at that as he pulled up to my house. I thanked him for the dinner and the ride. We exchanged numbers and said our goodbyes.

CHAPTER NINE
CHINK

I was on the couch, lying between Lah's legs and smiling from ear to ear, as we sat watching *The Seat Filler*. Yes, my boo passed with flying colors, and he wasn't pretending. He was enjoying the movie just as much as I was. DeRay Davis is hilarious, but I was trying to be cute, so I wasn't laughing aloud as much as I wanted to, but Lah was letting go. The movie was at my favorite part when Kelly Rowland is on stage singing, *I Need A Love*. Duane Martin stands up, holding the gardenia, and then all the seat fillers start to stand, holding their gardenias. I was trying not to tear up like I always did at this part of the movie. Just as my hand went up to wipe the tears that fell, the damn doorbell rang.

"Get the door, cry baby," Lah said, laughing.

"Oh, you saw that," I smiled.

"Yeah, I peeped it," he continued to laugh.

"Whatever," I said, mushing him in the head.

I got up to answer the door. I wasn't expecting anyone, so I didn't know who would be stopping by to interrupt movie night with my boo. I opened the door, and there was the same woman that was at my shop the other day, giving me the side eye. I was not in the mood for any female at my door talking about Lah is her man bullshit. That's the only reason I could think of for her being at my shop and now at my door.

"How may I help you?" I said, with my attitude on ten.

"Hello. First, I would like to apologize for just showing up at your door, but I really need to speak with you," she said, looking like she was about to cry.

"Ma'am, I don't even know you, so what could you possibly have to talk to me about?"

"Please. If you just allow me a few minutes of your time, I will explain."

"Give me a second," I said, closing the door.

I went back into the living room to speak with Lah because if this is his girlfriend, he has some explaining to do.

"Lah, there is a woman at the door that says she needs to speak with me. I told her to wait, because I wanted to give you the benefit of the doubt, so if you need to tell me something, you now have the floor," I said, holding my breath and hoping he didn't.

"If there's a woman at your door, I promise you she's not here about me. I only have you," he said as he got up to go to the door.

"Karen, what are you doing here?" he asked, and my heart dropped to the pit of my stomach.

"Hello, Lah. I didn't know you would be here. Like I told Chink, I didn't mean to intrude, but I need to speak with her."

I was a little confused. Shit, scratch that; I was a lot of confused. If she wasn't here about Lah, what the hell was she doing here, and how the hell did she know my name?

"Chink, this is the woman I was telling you about from my job," Lah said.

"Okay, but what does she need to speak with me about?" I asked.

"Well, there is only one way to find out," he said, letting her inside.

I sat on the couch, ready to go upside Lah's head. If this woman said anything pertaining to him, I swear I'm fucking both of them up. I looked over to him, but he didn't look nervous or anything, so I looked over to this woman named Karen. I was waiting for her to tell me what she came to tell me, but all she kept doing was wiping the tears that kept falling. Lah looked at me, and I looked at him, secretly saying to be ready to jump on her ass because she was looking real crazy right now.

"I'm sorry. Just give me a few minutes to get myself together," she cried.

"I'm going to need you to tell me what's going on. You're sitting here crying, but I don't know why," I said, getting impatient.

"Chink, I came here to tell you that I'm your birth mother," she blurted out, still crying.

I looked at this lady like she had really lost her mind; I couldn't believe that we let a psychopath into my home. She had to be crazy to be up in here talking about she's my mother. My mother was, and still is, Rita Montgomery.

"I'm going to have to ask you to leave because this isn't funny. My mom passed away, so for you to come here and play this game is sick," I said, standing up ready to pop her fucking head off.

"This isn't a joke, and all I ask is that you hear me out," she pleaded.

"Chink, come sit back down and hear what she has to say before you throw her out," Lah said, trying to be the voice of reason.

"As you already know, my name is Karen. When I was fifteen years old, I was dating my first love, Troy. Troy was Rita Montgomery's son, who was killed the same day that I was going to tell him that I was pregnant. Rita was mourning the death of her son, and I was mourning the death of my first love, so we leaned on each other. Being that my mom kicked me out of the house for getting pregnant, Rita told me that I could stay with her and she would help me raise her grandchild. I agreed because she said that she loved me as if I was her own daughter, and I believed her because I had no reason not to. Rita had other plans because when I went into labor, I begged her to take me to the hospital, but she kept assuring me that we had to wait until I was having contractions at least five minutes apart. I never made it to the hospital that day because Rita snatched my baby girl and left me for dead."

Karen paused for a few seconds to gather her thoughts and then continued. "I don't have all of the details of that night, but you're my daughter, and Rita was your grandmother. On the day that she was found murdered, I came here that morning and had a conversation with her about what she had done all those years ago. She begged me to leave well enough alone. I told her that I wasn't going to go to the authorities, but I was going to return that evening, and if she hadn't told you the truth, I was going to tell you. When I came back that evening, I found out that she was murdered, and I put off telling you to give you time to mourn."

"You really expect me to believe that my mom was my grandmother? What proof do you have?" I cried.

"The only physical evidence that I have is that you're the splitting image of your father, you have my eyes, and the fact that we can have a DNA test done," she said, handing me a picture that she took out of her purse.

I took the picture. The same picture sat on the mural in my mom's bedroom, along with a little girl's picture. I remembered how I used to ask my mom who the teenaged boy and the little girl in the picture were. She always told me that they were my brother and sister who died in a house fire. I believed her because I had no reason not to. There was no denying that I looked like the teenager in the picture, and I did have the same eyes as her, but that's not enough for me to believe her. Me looking like the teenager in the picture isn't news to me. My mother said he was my brother, so why wouldn't I look like him? As far as me having her eyes, shit, I've seen plenty of women with slanted eyes that had a chink to them. It didn't mean I was related to them.

I needed to call my aunt because if this lady was telling me the truth, somebody had to know something; and if this lady was a fraud, I needed my aunt to tell her to get out of my house and to stay the fuck away from me. Lah had an expression on his face that I couldn't read, but I could only imagine how I must look to him right now. I was a mess because no matter what I did, I couldn't stop the tears from falling, and I couldn't stop biting my nails.

"My mom said that this was my brother who passed away as a teenager. She had the same picture," I said, handing the picture back to her.

"I'm sorry she lied to you, but that's her son, Troy, your father in this picture," she said.

"I need to call my aunt. This is too much," I said with tears still falling.

"Sweetie, you can call your aunt, but I don't know if anyone else knew what your mom did all those years ago."

I ignored her and picked up my phone to call my Aunt Shirley. My hands were shaking so bad that I thought I was going to drop the phone.

"Hello," she answered.

"Aunt Shirley," I said, but that's all that I could get out as my lips trembled, and the tears continued to fall.

"Chink, what's going on? Why are you crying?" she asked with her voice full of worry.

I couldn't stop the tears, and once my body started to heave up and down, I was unable to speak. I handed the phone to Lah so that he could speak to her. I needed him let her know what was going on and to tell her that I needed her to come to the house.

"She said that she is on her way," he said, ending the call.

He said my aunt didn't give him a chance to say anything else after he mentioned Karen's name. She just told him she was on her way; it kind of made me think that she knew something. Lah tried to comfort me, but how can you comfort someone who just found out that her whole life might have been a lie? I got up, leaving Lah with my now unwanted guest, and I went to my mom's bedroom where everything remained the same. I sat on her bed; I felt her presence, and I could hear her voice telling me that if anything ever happened to her, not to let anyone tell me that she didn't love me and that everything she had done was for me. She used to say it so much, but now, it's starting to make sense; that was why she felt the need to

96

drill that into my head every chance that she got. I continued to sit, holding her picture in my hand with my tears falling.

My mom's door opened, and my Aunt Shirley came in, sat on the bed, and pulled me into her arms.

"Baby, look at me," she said with tears in her eyes.

I looked up at her, and my heart broke into tiny pieces because her eyes told me that she knew.

"Listen, baby, before you go being upset with me, I just want you to know that I only found out about what your mom had done after she passed away. When I was looking in her photo trunk to find a picture for the obituary, I found this journal at the bottom that gave all the details. I didn't tell you because I was going to let her secret die with her. She was your mom. She loved you, nurtured you, and protected you - that's what a mom does," she said.

"Auntie, this hurts so much. How could she take me and lie to me my entire life? She always taught me to be honest, no matter the consequences," I cried.

"Yes, she was teaching you to be a better version of herself. She made mistakes, and she didn't want you to make the same mistakes that she did."

"My whole life was a lie. There's no mistaking that. Now I have a stranger, that I don't know, who says she's my mother," I said, getting angry.

"Chink, your whole life wasn't a lie. We're still your blood family, and we always loved you. Had I known what my sister did, I wouldn't have let her raise you as her own. She had her reasons why she did what she did, and I'm not going to judge her just like I'm not going to make excuses for her. She's not here to defend her actions, so I will not allow anyone to bad mouth her. You were never abused and were always loved, and that's the memory I want you to remember," she said, no longer able to hold her tears back.

"I'm not judging her. I loved her when she was here and I still love her the same now that she's gone. It's just hard to swallow that the person who raised me to have morals and to respect others would snatch someone's child from them and raise the child as her own."

"Well, she wrote in the journal that she was going to tell you when you turned eighteen, but she never got the chance. So, she was going to tell you and share her reasons for why she felt the need to take you. Maybe you can speak with Karen; she may or may not be able to answer some of your questions. I don't know, but it's up to you if you want answers to any questions you may have. I sent her home because emotions are high, and if there is going to be a conversation, it's best to have that conversation another day. I took her number if you feel you want to move forward and have a DNA test done; it's your decision," she said, giving me the paper with Karen's number on it.

I walked my aunt out and told her that I loved her. I sat on the couch with a heavy heart; everybody's title in my family has shifted. Lah held me as I continued to cry, giving myself a banging headache. My Aunt Sherry called, but I just couldn't speak to her right now. I know that families have secrets, but when those secrets are exposed, I don't think that family should continue holding those secrets in. Somebody knew something; they just weren't saying what that something was.

I didn't even realize that Lah and I had fallen asleep until his phone vibrating against my hip woke me up. I wasn't going to wake him, but it kept going off back-to-back, so I figured it was an emergency.

"Lah, your phone is vibrating," I said as I shook him to wake him.

He looked at the phone and said it was Liem's mom calling. He missed the call, so he called her back.

"Mama D, I need you to slow down. Mama D, I'm on my way," I heard him yell into the phone.

"Chink, something went down with Liem. I couldn't understand what his mom was saying, so I have to head over there," he said with panic in his voice.

"Give me a few minutes. I'm going with you," I said.

That was the least I could have done. He was here with me in my time of need, and I felt the need to be with him so that I could offer him the same. I ran upstairs to brush my teeth and wash my face. I was still in my clothes from yesterday, but I didn't care as I grabbed my coat and hat out of the closet. We pulled up to Baisley Houses, and I hesitated because it was like three in the morning and mad niggas were chilling out front. Lah came around to my side and opened the door; he held my hand, and we walked up the walkway. I was shaking in my boots, but Lah made me feel safe, and he knew half of the dudes posted up anyway.

As soon as Mama D opened the door, she fell into Lah's arms, crying that someone shot her baby.

"Mama D, I need for you to calm down and tell me what's going on," Lah said as he walked her over to the couch to sit.

"Lahmiek, I got a call from a North Carolina police station. A detective was asking me a million questions about Liem, and after I told him that Liem was my son, he told me that he had been shot," she cried.

"Mama D, what the hell was Liem doing in North Carolina?" Lah asked her.

"Lahmiek, I don't know why he was in another state. All the detective said was he was shot, and he's at the county hospital. Well, that's the hospital I think he said. Cari wrote down the information," she cried.

I didn't even notice the little girl sitting at the kitchen table, crying silently. I put how I was feeling on the back burner as I went and tried to comfort her while Lah dealt with an inconsolable Mama D. Lah finally got her to go and lay down, and he tried to get a little more information about what was going on. I took Cari to her room and stayed with her until she drifted off to sleep. When I walked back into the living room, Lah was sitting on the couch with his head in his hands. He started to blame himself because he said that he knew that Liem was doing something that he wasn't supposed to be doing, but he didn't handle it like a big brother was supposed to. I just let him vent as I sat next to him and rested my head on his back, praying that his brother was going to be alright.

CHAPTER TEN

STEVEN

I walked in the house expecting my wife to be asleep, but she was sitting on the couch watching television. She never waits for me to get home, and now wasn't a good time because I didn't even wash my dick before leaving India's house. I was sweating bullets, hoping she didn't smell India's scent all over me.

"Babe, why you still up this late?" I asked, taking a seat on the other side of the room.

"Steven, I need to talk to you about something," she said, sniffing as if she had been crying.

I didn't need this bullshit, especially not tonight. Out of all nights that I walk my ass in the house after hours, she picks the one night I didn't wash my ass to want to wait on a nigga to talk.

"Babe, can this wait until morning after I get at least a couple of hours of sleep?" I asked her.

"If it could wait, do you think my ass would be up waiting to talk to you?" she yelled.

"Karen, look, I'm tired, and if all you want to do is argue, I can go to bed," I said.

"You can run the streets with a different hoe of the week, but you can't give me - your wife- a few minutes of your time? You know what? Go to fucking bed, Steven," she said, walking up the stairs.

I followed her up the stairs, but she wasn't in the bedroom, so I decided to go and take a shower and then go and try to mend her attitude. I knew sooner or later she was going to get tired of me running the streets and coming in at all hours of the night, but I had no idea tonight would be the night she chose to talk about it. I was just praying that she wouldn't ask me for a divorce because like I said before, I love her, and I'm not trying to lose her. I know it sounds selfish, but it is what it is.

When I came out of the bathroom, I saw that Karen was in the bed. I thought that maybe she was lying in bed awake, but as I got closer, I could hear her snoring lightly. I wasn't ready to go to bed just yet; I know I told my wife I was tired, but that was just to give me time to wash off India's scent. I went downstairs to watch television, but as soon as I got comfortable on the couch, watching ESPN and enjoying a Coors Light, my phone alerted me that I had a text message.

India: Hey, Steven. I'm sorry to be texting you this late, but I'm in a lot of pain and need to go to the hospital.

I don't have anyone to take me or sit with Tahira while I'm being seen.

Me: India, why would you text me? Put down the phone and call 911 if you're in that much pain.

India: If I could have called 911, I wouldn't be texting you asking you to come. I told you that I don't have anyone to sit with your daughter.

Me: I can't come to take you to the hospital because I just got home, and the wife is still up. I know she doesn't want to hear that I'm leaving the house again this late.

India: Steven, I don't ask for much, and if I didn't really need you, I wouldn't be asking you. Please, I have no one else to call.

Me: Look, India, all I can tell you is to call a cab and have a nurse look after Tahira while you're being seen.

India: Really? So you feel comfortable with someone else looking after your daughter? I swear, the one time I really need you, and this is how you do me. I swear your punk ass will regret your fucking decision not to come in my time of need. You don't care about your fucking daughter or me. Mark my words that I'm going to show you that I don't care about you or your fucking marriage either.

I didn't even bother to respond as I turned my phone off and continued watching television and enjoying my beer. I don't know how many times I have to instill in her that she isn't my woman, and to be honest, I hope the bitch was having a miscarriage because that would be one less problem I had to deal with. I woke up the next morning to twenty messages from India, but I refused to call or text her back. I heard Karen moving around in the kitchen, so I headed upstairs to brush my teeth and wash my face so that we could talk. When I got back downstairs, Karen was sitting at the table, drinking a cup of coffee.

"Good morning," I said, kissing her on the cheek.

"Good morning," she replied smugly.

"I just want to apologize for last night, and if you still want to talk, I'm all ears," I said, hoping she didn't.

"You sure you have time?" she asked sarcastically.

"I'm willing to make time for my beautiful wife," I said, and she rolled her eyes.

"What I wanted to talk to you about last night was us not having any children and the real reason that I have been unable to conceive," she said.

I know it may sound mean, but why in the fuck do I want to talk about some shit that isn't going to change anything? I have come to accept that we will never have children, so I really wasn't in the mood to keep reliving this bullshit. I swear if I had any inclination that this was what she wanted to talk about, I would have just took my ass to work and left her ass mad at me.

"Steven, I never shared with anyone that when I was fifteen years old, I was pregnant with my boyfriend Troy's baby."

"Pregnant? What? How?" I asked. I was confused because she'd told me that she was never able to conceive.

"Steven, please let me finish. I was pregnant at the age of fifteen, and when my mother found out, she kicked me out of the house. I packed my things to go to Troy's, but when I got to his house, his mother answered the door crying. That same day that I went to share my news of being pregnant with his child is the day I found out that he was killed. His mother took me in, pretending to care for me, but like I said, I was only fifteen, and young and dumb at the time. I didn't know that she had plans on snatching my baby and leaving me for dead, but that's exactly what she did. Losing so much blood resulted in me having complications, and that's the reason that caused me not to have any more children."

"So you hid this knowing how much I wanted children before we married?" I asked.

"Steven, when we married, I didn't know that I wouldn't be able to have any children. I learned of the condition I have at the same time you did - when the doctor told us. When he told us that I had Premature Ovarian Insufficiency and that the exact cause was unknown, that's when I knew that the complications from my first pregnancy caused it or played some part in it," she said, crying.

We've been married all these years, and she didn't feel the need to tell me about what happened to her. That's not something you keep from your husband, so why the fuck should I care about it now?

"Steven, I know that you don't care about it at this point, and I know that I should have told you about what happened to me, but at the time, I just wanted to leave it in my past," she cried out as if she knew what I was thinking.

"You're right, that's exactly how I feel. You didn't feel the need to share this with me all those years ago, so why now?"

"I'm telling you now because a few years ago, I started looking for my daughter's grandmother with the help of a private investigator, and after two long years, he finally found her," she said, now smiling.

"And you didn't think this was something that you share with your husband?" I said, getting upset at how selfish she's been.

"Steven, I didn't want to share this with you until I found out something because it wouldn't have made sense to share if I had nothing to share."

"No, what you mean is that if the investigator didn't find anything, you would have continued to keep it to yourself, taking it to your grave. Right?"

"Look, Steven, that's not the case. Anyway, I went to the address that the investigator gave me, and I approached Troy's mother and told her that she had until the end of that day to tell her granddaughter that I was her biological mother. Long story short, when I returned to finally meet my daughter, someone had murdered her grandmother."

"Whoa, hold up because this shit is sounding crazier by the minute. Did you have something to do with her being murdered?" I asked her.

"Steven, you know damn well that I'm not capable of murdering anyone."

"I don't know too much of anything about the woman I've been married to for over ten years; I can't believe that she would keep something like this from her husband," I said, being honest.

"Well no, I didn't kill her Steven, but I did fall back from telling my daughter that I was her mother until a few days ago. I went to her home and told her that I was her biological mother."

"And?"

"And she didn't believe me. She called her aunt, who asked me to leave and told me that if my daughter wanted to contact me, she would give her the number to do so, but as of today, she hasn't called."

I just sat for a few minutes, trying to take all of this in. This was some shit that you see in a movie, not in real life. Karen got me fucked up if she thinks that I'm just going to accept it now that she's decided to be honest.

"Karen, this is real selfish of you, keeping this secret all these years, and now you just expect me to accept a fucking daughter after you denied me of being with someone who could have given me children."

"Steven, that's not fair. You should know that if I didn't tell you it was because I didn't know how to tell you," she said, getting angry.

"Karen, I really don't know what you expect me to say or how you expected me to feel."

"I want you to say that if my daughter wants to be a part of my life then you will support my decision of getting to know my daughter and accept her into our family."

"Just fucking selfish. I don't believe you right now. You tell me this bullshit and offer no apology, but I have to sit here and just fucking accept it."

"Steven, don't go there because this hasn't been some fairytale marriage, and you haven't been my husband for years. I know about all the women you parade around with; just like I hired an investigator to find my daughter, I hired one to follow your ass," she said with her hand on her hip. "So you've got nothing to say now? Next time you decide to point your accusatory finger at me, just remember that I'm not the only one with secrets."

"I haven't been unfaithful in this marriage, Karen, just unhappy," I lied.

"Really? So the call I got last night, waking me up out of my sleep, from someone named India, telling me she has a child by you and one on the way, isn't true?" she asked through her tears.

So that little bitch called my wife. I didn't think the bitch had it in her, but I was wrong. I could deny it, but why should I? 'This whole marriage has been a lie,' I thought as I came out swinging.

"Fair exchange is no robbery, so don't sit here and try to call me out about possibly having two children," I said, knowing I was dead wrong.

"Steven, me having a child when I was fifteen is hardly the same as you stepping outside of this marriage, sleeping with another woman, and fathering children!" she screamed and slapped the shit out of me.

"That was real adult of you, Karen," I said, holding my face.

"Fuck you, Steven. So it's true you have fucking kids. You bastard," she cried, trying to hit me again.

I grabbed both of her hands, warning her not to put her fucking hands on me again. I could see the hurt in her eyes. What the fuck did she expect me to do? She's been in this marriage physically for years, but her mind, body, and soul have been somewhere else. Now I know what kept her from giving me her all. She was too occupied with losing her daughter and trying to reconnect with her all these years. How do you marry someone that you don't love enough to tell them that part of your life? I wasn't going to stand here and continue a conversation that was becoming physical because if Karen put her hands on me one more time, I couldn't promise that I wouldn't knock her on her ass. I went back upstairs to get dressed so I could go and check this bitch India before taking my ass to work.

CHAPTER ELEVEN

LAH

I walked into the poolroom looking for Drone. After finding out from Liem that he was trafficking for Drone, I was pissed. Drone was standing against the wall with a cue stick in one hand and a beer in the other. I didn't want to make a scene, so I had to be cool with my approach.

"What's up, Drone? Let me holla at you."

"'I'll holla at you after this game, man," he said, not even looking at me.

"Look bro, I need to holla at you now," I said. I was trying to remain calm because clearly, he was trying to play me.

"Playboy, be easy. I said I'll holla at you after this game. These youngins nowadays have no respect for their elders," he said. He was talking to me but co-signing with some dude posted up next to him.

No longer able to control my anger, I grabbed a cue stick and beat him with it repeatedly until someone pulled me off his punk ass. He was lying on the floor, leaking from his nose and mouth.

"I told your bitch-made ass that my brother was off limits, you fucking punk," I said, hitting him again.

One of his fake thugs tried to flex on me, and before he could make a move, he was staring down the barrel of my gun. I pointed it at him, daring his bitch ass to make a move.

"I advise you to back the fuck up before your blood decorates these walls. This shit here has nothing to do with your ass, but if you want to take a bullet for this punk, continue to flex," I said, still pointing the gun.

The bitch that Drone was with helped him up off the floor, and he was still talking shit as if he didn't just get his old ass beat.

"So you're a tough guy, huh?" he asked as he spit blood onto the floor.

"It's not about being tough. You got my brother caught up after I told you that he was off limits, then you didn't even have the decency to see if he was okay."

"He's a grown ass man. He approached me, so who am I to stop a man from trying to get this money?"

"I see how you want to play. Stay the fuck away from my brother because if I find out you even looked at him wrong, your ass is dead," I threatened him.

"I don't think you're in any position to make threats. I'm sure that you don't want your little girlfriend to find out who you really are, so fuck with me if you want to. And that's not a threat; it's a promise."

I swear that if there weren't any witnesses, I would have killed him where he stood. I lowered my gun and turned to leave with this motherfucker still talking shit.

"Tell your punk ass brother that he owes me for my shit that he lost," he laughed.

'This faggot has lost his fucking mind,' I thought as I rushed his ass, knocking him out cold with the butt of my gun. I'm hoping that he got the message that I am my brother's keeper, and all debts are paid and void as I backed out of the pool hall to my car. Someone shot Liem in the back and left him for dead, and this motherfucker is trying to hold some fucking drugs over his head. On my dead grandmother, if that faggot ass nigga even looks at my brother wrong, it's lights out for his ass. And then his bitch ass had the nerve to say that he was going to tell Chink my secret, so he'll be lucky if his ass sees his next birthday, being a snitch-ass nigga.

I drove straight home because that's how pissed I was. I told Mama D that I would come by to see Liem, but I just wanted to go home and get this blood off me. I wanted to take a hot shower, have a drink, and call it a night. The stress of Drone threatening to tell Chink what I planned on taking to my grave was now taking a toll on me as my head began banging. I tried to tell myself that it was just business, and it had nothing to do with her or against her, because I didn't even know her like that at the time. It didn't make me feel any less guilty, and I had to decide whether to tell her or to take out the only person that knows of what I did.

That shower was everything. It washed away some of the stress that I was feeling, and I was now sitting on my bed, throwing back shots of Hennessy and trying not to think about it. I called Liem to make sure that he was okay and promised him that I would stop by tomorrow when I got off work. I decided to call and talk to Chink because she always makes me feel better even on my worst days. She convinced me to come and spend the night with her. I knew that I shouldn't be driving after all the shots that I just had, but it wouldn't be the first time. I grabbed my keys and headed out the door.

STEVEN

I got out of my car and headed toward India's house. I took a few deep breaths, trying to calm down before seeing her. I knocked on the door, but there was no answer. I was turning to walk back to my car, but I stopped when I heard movement inside. I decided to turn the doorknob, and the door opened. I walked inside and saw India sitting on the floor with her back against the wall. She had this strange look on her face, and her clothes were wet.

"India, what's going on with you?" I asked her.

"Please, don't come here like you care now, Steven. Where were you when I needed you?" she cried out.

"India, I told you that I couldn't leave the house last night, but I'm here now."

"Steven, it's too late. You never loved me like I loved you. No matter how much I tried to show you, it was never enough. All you have ever done was sell me a dream, but you're nothing but a fucking dream killer. You never had any plans on leaving your wife for me!" she said. She continued to cry, and she was now rocking back and forth.

"India, you know my situation is complicated, and I can't just leave," I lied.

"Stop fucking lying, Steven! You made me love you, knowing that I wasn't enough to make you leave. Hell, your fucking daughter wasn't even enough to make you leave. All I ever wanted was for you to love me and your daughter the same way we loved you," she cried.

"India, let's be real; I had doubts about Tahira being my daughter. I wasn't the only person that you were dealing with, so don't act as if you were home waiting on a nigga," I said, getting upset because she was playing victim.

"Steven, it doesn't even matter anymore. I no longer have anything that belongs to you. You're free to go and live your miserable life with your miserable marriage," she yelled.

"What the fuck are you talking about? So now, are you telling me that she isn't my fucking daughter after all this time?" I asked her.

"I called you, Steven. I texted you over and over again, and you ignored me. I even called your wife, thinking that if she got upset with you, it would cause an argument. I thought that you would come, and even if it was just to curse me out, at least you would have been here. But no, you never came, so I had to sit here and go through all this pain alone, losing my fucking baby in the process," she said, pointing between her legs.

I didn't even notice that her pants were stained with blood when I first walked in, but now, looking at her pajama pants, I felt bad. She was now crying hysterically, and I didn't know what to say or do.

"I lost my baby because of you, Steven. Why didn't you just come and take me to the hospital?" she said, almost in a childlike whisper.

I walked over to her to try and help her up off the floor so that I could help her get cleaned up and take her to the hospital. She looked so broken, and it was beginning to bother me that I ignored her calls. I even felt bad for wishing that she would have a miscarriage.

"India, come on and let me help you so that I can take you to the hospital," I said with all the compassion that I could muster up.

"Help me! It's a little too late to help me, Steven. Both of my babies are dead, and it's all your fault!" she screamed.

It took me a few seconds to register that she said both her babies. What the fuck did she mean by both her babies are dead?

"India, what are you talking about? Where is Tahira?" I asked. My voice was cracking, and I was beginning to panic.

She just looked at me and continued to cry as she rocked back and forth. I stood from the kneeling position that I was in and started up the stairs to look for Tahira. She wasn't in any of the bedrooms, so I went into the direction of the bathroom, and nothing could have prepared me for what I was looking at. I was momentarily stuck in place as I looked at her tiny body floating face down in a tub of water. I quickly recovered, pulling her out of the bathtub, and trying to resuscitate her to no avail. I pulled out my phone and dialed 911 to let them know that I needed them to send an ambulance. Looking at my baby girl, lying there lifeless, did something to my mental. All of the feelings that I'd tried to hide because I didn't want to get caught up if she wasn't mine came full force as I cried for her.

I felt something that I never felt before as I rushed back downstairs to where India was still rocking back and forth. Unable to control myself, and with tears pouring from my eyes, I grabbed India, shaking her and asking her why. She just looked up at me with pained eyes, but her pained eyes didn't mean anything to me. I blacked out, grabbed her around her neck, and squeezed until she was no longer moving. I stood up and backed away from her, realizing what I'd just done. I had to get out of there. I ran out of the house, jumped into my car, and drove off, just as the ambulance was pulling up.

I ended up on the shoulder of the Grand Central Parkway on the side of Flushing Meadows Park. I sat in my car, asking God for forgiveness for all of my sins as the tears continued to fall from my eyes. I briefly thought about my wife and all the women that I had deceived as I leaned toward my glove compartment. I knew that I wasn't built to sit in anybody's jail for the rest of my life. I reached my hand into the glove compartment and took out my gun, putting it to my head. I said a silent prayer before pulling the trigger.

CHAPTER TWELVE
CHINK

Lah was at my house pretending that nothing was bothering him, but I knew that it was because he wasn't his normal upbeat self. I wanted to talk to him about setting up a meeting with Karen so that I could finally have a sit down with her to get her side of what happened all those years ago. Even though it wouldn't change the fact that Rita Montgomery was my mother, I still wanted to hear the story from her point of view. I went to my visit my mom at her gravesite to let her know that I loved her and forgave her. At first, I wanted to be mad at her, but I just couldn't because, no matter the situation, she had always been there for me and treated me as her child, loving me unconditionally.

"Hey, do you want to talk about it?" I asked Lah.

"I'm good. Just worried about my brother," he said.

"How is he feeling? Polo wanted me to ask you if it would be okay if she visited him."

"Let me find out little mama feeling my brother," he laughed.

"They had a brief interaction, not on some 'I want to be your man' type of thing, but he did promise to take her out just before he got shot."

"Word? We need to set that meeting up. Maybe she can get him out of his funk and up out of that bed," he said.

"Okay, I'm going to talk to Polo to see when is a good time for her, and I need you to set up the meeting with Karen. I'm ready."

"Cool. What's for dinner in this joint?" he asked, rubbing his stomach and laughing.

"Um, you can go into the kitchen, and the drawer next to the stove has all kinds of takeout menus. Take your pick," I laughed, but I was dead ass serious. I was not cooking.

"So that's how you do me?" he asked, pulling me into his lap and kissing me.

Lah's tongue danced around in my mouth, causing me to let out a low moan. I straddled him, grinding my hips into him as he continued to suck on my tongue. I could feel myself on the verge of an orgasm, and it wasn't the kind that I have when I'm in the bathroom pleasuring myself while thinking of him. This one was different. My hips moved faster, and I dry humped him until I released.

My movement slowed down and embarrassment took over as I excused myself.

I heard Lah come into the bathroom just as I stepped into the shower. I had just started to wash myself, trying to keep my tears of embarrassment from falling, when I felt his hand on my lower back, asking me to face him. I turned to look at him, and my eyes got big. I was thinking to myself that this nigga was crazy as I looked down. He was now standing in the tub, fully dressed. He was getting wet as he lifted my chin so that I was now looking up at him.

"Chink, I want to apologize for what happened downstairs. I got caught up in the moment, and I don't want you to feel no kind of way about having an orgasm with your clothes still on," he joked, making me smile.

"You don't have to apologize. If I didn't want to dry hump you, I wouldn't have. I got caught up in the moment too, and I was embarrassed at having an orgasm with my clothes still on. That's why I excused myself," I said, being honest.

"Nah, you have no reason to be embarrassed. It is what it is," he said, kissing me.

We stood in the shower continuing to kiss each other, and I got lost in the moment once again, not caring that he was seeing me butt ass naked as I began to help him remove his wet clothes, piece by piece. Once he stood naked as the day he was born, I couldn't help but to get lost staring at the chocolate thickness that had my mouth watering. He put my right leg up on the side of the tub and starting kissing the inside of my thigh. My body was on fire as I anticipated his lips between my legs. I grabbed his head with one hand and held onto the wall with my other hand as his lips made contact with my clit. I let out a loud moan as I fucked his face, feeling another orgasm coming. He reached around and started fingering my asshole, taking me over the top as my juices flowed just like the water from the showerhead flowed. It was definitely a downpour as he sucked, licked, and swallowed every drop. He turned me around to face the wall as he deep tongued my asshole. My legs went weak as I did everything in my power not to fall; instead, I tried to enjoy the ride. I have never had dick before, but if this man had me feeling like this with his tongue, I was ready to feel what ride his dick was going to take me on.

After I slowly began to come off my high, we washed and continued what we started in the bedroom. He grabbed a condom but not before asking me for the third time if I was sure that I was ready. We both knew that once I gave up my virginity there was no getting it back, so I respected that he thought enough of me to even ask; most guys wouldn't have given a shit. I shook my head that I was sure as I felt the tip of his dick at my opening. I closed my eyes, expecting to feel a great deal of pain, but he was gentle. He started slowly, inch by inch, until all of him was inside of me. I felt some pain, but as I started to match him stroke for stroke, I began to feel an indescribable feeling as my hands reached behind him, grabbing his butt and helping him pump into me with deep, long strokes. He flipped me on top, and since I've never had sex before, I just closed my eyes, held onto his chest, and mimicked what I saw the women do in the movies on After Dark on HBO. I must have been doing something right because his moans were matching my own.

Lah worked me in every position known, and he had my kitty hurting something good. My first time was well worth the wait. We now lay in each other's arms, drunk off our lovemaking session. Lah was snoring lightly, but sleep wouldn't find me any time soon because I couldn't sleep after experiencing the best night of my life. To hear him tell me that he loved me had me on a high that I didn't want to come off of just yet. I didn't want to fall asleep, just to wake up thinking I'd dreamed it all, so I'm just going to lay here and bask in the moment. I wanted to call Polo, but it was like three in the morning. I knew that she would pick up, because that is how we do, but I didn't want to wake her just to tell her that Lah put it on me. I'll just keep my excitement to myself until I spoke to her later on. I felt kind of crazy because I couldn't stop smiling, but after a while, I started to realize that what goes up must come down as my high came all the way down. I started thinking that maybe he just said that he loves me because we were having a lovemaking moment. 'Why do I always do this to myself?' I thought as I put my head on his chest and fell asleep in self-doubt.

LAH

I walked down the stairs quietly, trying not to wake Chink just yet, because I wanted to surprise her with breakfast in bed. I opened the refrigerator to get the things that I needed to make her an omelet. I tried to shake off the bad vibe that I was feeling as I moved about in the kitchen. I grabbed two glasses out of the cabinet, filled them both with orange juice, and placed them on the tray.

Just as I got to the top of the stairs, I heard someone knocking on the front door. 'Damn,' I thought as I carried the tray back downstairs and sat it down on the kitchen table before answering the door. I opened the door to a crying Karen, standing on the doorstep once again. I invited her in, and she apologized for just showing up uninvited again. She asked for Chink, and I told her to give me a few minutes. I just hoped that Chink didn't flip on her because even though Chink was ready to meet with her, Karen didn't know that, and her just showing up might piss Chink off. Chink was coming out of the bathroom when I got back up the stairs. I gave her a kiss, and I'm not going to lie, I was a little pissed off that Karen ruined my boo's breakfast in bed this morning.

"Good morning. Who was at the door?" she asked me.

"It's Karen, and she doesn't look good," I answered.

"Did she say what she wanted this time?" she asked.

"No, she's crying and didn't say much of anything; she just asked if she could speak to you."

Chick rolled her eyes as she put on a pair of jeans and a t-shirt before heading downstairs. I said a silent prayer that Chink didn't go off on her. I followed her into the living room, and I could tell that once she saw Karen, her face softened.

"I'm sorry to once again stop by without your permission, but I had nowhere else to go, and I just didn't feel like being alone. I just got a call this morning that my husband's body was found in his car and that they need me to come down and identify his body," she cried.

Chink went to sit next to her, and she held Karen's hands as she continued.

"We had an argument the night before that spilled over to the next morning, so when he left for work, we weren't even on speaking terms. Now I will never get the chance to tell him how much I love him and how sorry I am for the part that I played in the argument," she cried.

"I'm sure he knows how much you loved him. One argument didn't change that; I'm sorry that you lost your husband, and if you need anything, I'm here," Chink said.

"Again, I apologize and thank you for understanding. Like I said, I really didn't have anywhere else to turn. I'm not trying to be a burden on you, it's just that I'm also having a hard time because the officer said that my husband took his own life, but my husband would never take his own life. The argument wasn't that serious or at least I didn't think it was," she said.

"Listen, why don't you try to calm down? I'm going to make you some tea, and as soon as you feel up to going to identify your husband's body, I will drive you myself," Chink said, getting up to go into the kitchen with me following behind her.

As soon as I walked in behind her, I saw her wipe away tears that had fallen. I wrapped her in a bear hug from behind, asking her if she was okay. She said that she was as I let her go.

"Oh, you made me breakfast?" she asked, looking at the tray on the table.

"Yes, it was my little surprise before the knock at the door. I wanted to give you breakfast in bed to show you how much I appreciate and love you for trusting me to be your first," I said, meaning every word.

"Awww, I love you too, Lah, and I wouldn't have had it any other way. Last night was perfect," she said, kissing me.

I sat at the table watching her as she made Karen's tea. I really lucked up and met the perfect woman, but it scared me to my core that I could lose her at any given moment if what happened in the dark came to light.

CHAPTER THIRTEEN
CHINK

I just got back from going with Karen to identify her husband's body, and I really felt bad for her because I knew all too well how it felt to lose someone you love. We stopped by the police station to speak to the detective that requested that she come down to the station. The case is still under investigation; even though they are ruling his death a suicide, they now believe him to be connected in some way to the murder of his daughter and her mother. Karen insisted that her husband wasn't capable of murder. She was a mess, so I offered for her to come back to the house and she accepted.

She was now upstairs in my room resting. I had to make sure that I changed the sheets and sprayed the room before allowing her to enter because she didn't need to know what took place the night before. Just thinking about it gave me a tingling sensation between my legs. I sent Lah a text to let him know that I was back in the house and that Karen was in my room resting. I closed my shop for the rest of the week, canceling all appointments and giving the stylists the week off, letting them know that I had death in the family. No, he wasn't related to me, but I wanted to be here for her because she didn't have anyone. My phone alerted me that Lah texted me back.

Lah: Hey, how is Karen holding up?

Me: She's having a hard time coming to grips with what she learned today.

Lah: I heard. Shit's got me bugging right now because the woman that they claim to have been her husband's baby's mama is a chick that I used to kick it with, and I didn't even know she had a kid.

Me: Really? This whole story is crazy and doesn't make any sense. Why would he kill the baby, her mother, and then himself? Something just doesn't add up here.

Lah: Well hopefully that wasn't the case, but I have to get back to work. Let Karen know that everyone at work sends their love, and I will see you later on tonight.

Me: Okay. TTYL.

I finished texting Lah, and then I googled NY1 to read the news article and to see if they had a picture of the woman that was murdered. I wasn't interested in reading the article or seeing the news report until Lah said that he used to kick it with ole girl. I wanted to see what she looked like. Petty I know, but I couldn't help myself. As soon as the article loaded, I heard a knock on the door, so I had to put my phone down and look at it later.

133

I opened the door and it was Polo, standing there with red eyes like she had been crying, I stepped to the side, letting her in with concern written all over my face. I was hoping that it wasn't bad news because I had enough bad news for one day.

Polo went to sit on the couch and laid her head back, silently crying. I waited a few minutes, but it didn't look as if she was going to offer me any explanation as to what was wrong with her, so I asked her.

"Polo, are you going to tell me what's wrong?"

She looked up at me with tears in her eyes, and I'm telling you, anyone who has a best friend knows that it doesn't matter what the reason is, if you see them hurting, you automatically hurt right along with them. That's exactly what happened to me as I wiped my own tears, trying to remind myself that I needed to be as strong for her as she has always been for me.

"Chink, I just found out that Steven is dead. I went to the police station trying to get information to find out if it was true, but being I wasn't family, I wasn't able to get any information," she cried.

She noticed that I didn't say anything, and she was looking at me with questioning eyes, but I couldn't speak. I felt lightheaded as it began to register that her Steven and Karen's Steven were one and the same. I never got the chance to meet Steven because he backed out of Christmas dinner at the last minute, so I had no idea what he even looked like. This shit is crazy, and now I have to tell my best friend that Steven did indeed have a wife like she thought all along, and his wife is the woman who is claiming to be my biological mother, and she is upstairs resting in my bed. Even though she'd stopped dating him, I know the blow isn't going to hurt any less, and I needed to be careful how I delivered it.

"Polo, I don't know how to tell you this, but I already know about what happened to Steven. You remember Karen, the woman who I told you is claiming to be my biological mother? She was his wife. I promise you that I had no idea that her Steven was the same Steven that you were dating until you mentioned that your Steven passed on. She came over here because she didn't have anywhere else to go, and she's upstairs right now lying down," I said.

"So he was married, damn. I knew it; why couldn't he just tell me the truth?" she said, more to herself than to me.

"Polo, I'm so sorry you had to find out like this because I know how you felt about him," I stuttered a little.

I was scared to ask her if she had heard the story that the news was reporting about him supposedly killing his daughter and her mother.

"Polo, how did you find out about Steven?" I asked her.

"My classmate told me that she heard about it on the news, and when she told me, I had to leave school because I got sick to my stomach. I didn't want to believe it. So like I said, I went to the police station, and when they wouldn't confirm anything for me, I googled it," she said, wiping her eyes.

"So you know that they are trying to say that he killed his daughter, her mother, and himself?" I asked.

"Yes, I read the news report, but I don't believe it. I can honestly believe the part about him having a daughter, and I can even believe that he was still dating the mother, but killing them? I don't believe it. The article didn't even mention that he was married, so that shows that they don't have all the facts in this case," she cried.

"All I know is that this shit is crazy; my best friend and the woman who claims to be my mother were in love with the same damn man. I need a drink," I said seriously.

Polo smiled through her tears. I'm glad that I was able to make her smile at a time like this, but my ass was dead serious. I needed a fucking drink ASAP because this shit was unbelievable and hard to swallow.

"I'm going to need you and Karen to be cool because both of you were deceived by Steven," I said.

"Chink, this shit hurts like hell, but believe me when I say that I have no beef with his wife. I knew that something was up with him, and I'm just glad that I did the right thing and left him alone because I would never intentionally break up anyone's home," she said.

"Polo, I know that you're not that type of person, and I'm sure Karen can respect the fact that you stopped seeing him when you suspected that he was married. I can only imagine what Karen is feeling right now. Not only is her husband dead, but she had to find out that he was living another whole life."

I walked over to give my friend a hug just as Karen was making her way downstairs into the living room.

"How are you feeling?" I asked her.

"I feel like I'm stuck in a dream and haven't awakened yet," she responded, looking at Polo strangely.

"I'm sorry, excuse my manners. This is my best friend, Polo, and Polo, this is Karen," I said nervously.

"Not to be rude, but I know who she is. I know her as Patricia, and she's one of the women that my husband cheated on me with," she said.

I didn't know that she knew beforehand that her husband was cheating on her; I thought that she just found out when she heard the news report, but boy, was I wrong. She informed us that she hired a private investigator to follow her husband, who had numerous women. I made sure to express to her that Polo didn't know that he was married, and as soon as she suspected that he was, she left him alone. She said that her husband had been dating women half his age for the past few years, and she never left him because she didn't want to be alone. I'm just glad that she didn't flip out on Polo because I would have had to let her know that it wasn't going down like that, especially not in my home. I've known Polo all my life; she was the sister I never had, and I've only known Karen for a few weeks. I wouldn't let her disrespect my friend because her beef should have been with her husband.

Strangely, Polo and Karen put their feelings aside, and we were now at the dining room table, helping her with the arrangements for her husband. Polo was happy that Karen allowed her to be a part of the planning for Steven's home going ceremony. I knew that this was hard for Karen, but I guess she figured he was gone, so there was no reason to have ill feelings toward Polo.

Polo left about seven that evening, agreeing to meet up with Lah and me at Liem's house tomorrow. Karen and I were wrapping up the last page of the obituary when Lah got to the house. Karen said that she was leaving to go home, and I insisted that she stay because I knew that she wasn't ready to go home just yet. She declined, and I knew it had to do with her not wanting to intrude being that Lah was now here. I respected her decision and told her to call me if she needed me. I locked the door, joined Lah on the couch, and let the day's events leave my body so that I could focus on my man.

CHAPTER FOURTEEN

POLO

It's been a few months, and I was finally over my depression stage. I didn't realize how much I really cared for Steven until he was gone. It was easy not seeing him because of the break up, and I knew that he would eventually call or pop up at my school without notice. But now, the reality of him really being gone was too much to handle. I have been kicking it with Liem for about a month, and we have been inseparable. If I wasn't at school or work, I was with him and his family, chilling at their house. I hardly had time to spend with Chink anymore, and I was missing my best friend. Between her spending time with Lah and getting to know Karen, my time with her has been limited. They finally got the DNA test done, and it confirmed that Karen was her biological mother.

I was standing outside of my school, waiting on Liem to pick me up. Lah purchased him a ride; it was nothing fancy, just something to get him back and forth between work and home. He has been saving and planning on upgrading. He was taking me to Red Lobster; this would be our official dinner date, being we never got to have the one that he promised me just before he was shot. I'm happy that he recovered, and that part of his life is over. He's working at the same hospital as Lah, in the mailroom. It wasn't his dream job, but he had to start somewhere. Lah talked his mother into getting him the job because he didn't want Liem to feel that he had to go back to doing any illegal activities to support his family.

Dinner was going great, and our conversation was flowing. We were really enjoying each other's company, like we always have, until that trick, Nailah, walked over. She was being rude as if I wasn't even sitting at the table.

"So, I guess this is the reason you decided not to return any of my calls?" she asked Liem.

"Nailah, I didn't return any of your calls because our last interaction didn't end well," he answered.

"Well, I wasn't calling to catch up on our last interaction; I was calling to check on you after you got shot."

"I appreciate the love, but now is not the time. As you can see, I'm out on a date with my girl," he said, looking at me.

"Let's not get cute in front of your ugly, little girlfriend. Don't sit there and act like you weren't sweating me," she said.

I looked at this bitch like, no she didn't. It was no denying that she was bad, but this white girl was just as bad. Her trying to play me in front of Liem just let me know that she was threatened by me. I was about to say something to let her know that I get down with the best of them, but I didn't have to because Liem checked her ass, and she walked back over to her table, pissed off.

"I'm sorry about that. Her ass is tripping, coming over here on that bullshit," he said.

"I'm not even sweating her ass. That trick has been hating on Chink and I since high school," I said.

"It still doesn't give her the right to come over here, trying to flex when she didn't care shit about me. The only thing that she cared about was what I could do for her ass."

"That didn't stop your ass from trying to trick on that hoe when you knew what she was about," I said, regretting it as soon as the words left my mouth.

I didn't want him to see that I was feeling some kind of way about him trying to get with her. I'm not usually the jealous type, but something about Liem hooking up with that trick had me bothered.

"Do I hear a little jealousy over there? Trust, you have nothing to worry about. I'm with who I'm trying to be with," he said.

"Trust and believe, I'm not jealous," I lied.

"Well, like I said, you have no reason to be jealous because the person I'm trying to be with is sitting across from me. So, what would you say if I asked you to be my girl?" he asked.

"Wow, so you're going to just put me on the spot at the restaurant?" I laughed; it was something I did when I was nervous.

"It shouldn't matter if I asked you at the grocery store. You should know if you're feeling me enough to know if you want to be my girl or not," he said.

"Liem, I don't mind seeing where this can go, but I have to stress that nothing or no one is more important than me finishing school," I said seriously.

"I would never ask or expect you to put me before school. What kind of man would I be to ask that of you?"

"I'm not saying that you would, but I just feel the need to put it on the table," I smiled, letting him know I meant no harm.

"Okay, so now that we have that on the table, and now off the table, will you be my girl and my girl only?" he asked, now holding my hands from across the table.

"Yes, I will be your girl, Liem, if you will be my man, and my man only," I said, and we both laughed.

We just stared at each other for a few moments before he leaned toward me from across the table for what would have been our first kiss, but the hater was back. I really started to believe she was begging to be fucked up. Why couldn't she keep her ass at the table with her ratchet-ass friends? I don't know if it was them, who were putting the battery in her back, but if she knew what I knew, she would go back to her table and leave well enough alone. I never understood females who only wanted the man when he started seeing or showing interest in someone else. Liem was hers for the taking, but all she saw was dollar signs. Now, all of a sudden, she feels the need to hate. I took a deep breath before speaking because I didn't want to make a scene at the restaurant, but I needed her to leave.

"Nailah, is there something we can do for you?" I asked, not masking how upset I was that she interrupted me feeling Liem's soft lips on mine.

"Please shut the fuck up. I'm sure you were taught to speak when spoken to," she had the nerve to say.

"Nailah, you have two seconds to get the fuck away from this table," I said.

Nailah just took me to a place she had no idea that I could go. Growing up in Queens was hard as hell with those hating ass females always sleeping on the white girl. I had to prove myself day in and day out until those bitches respected me. Now here was this bitch, trying me. I didn't want to have to show out in front of Liem, but it was bound to happen if her ass didn't take a walk away from this table.

The waitress approached the table to ask if we needed anything else, and I told her that we needed our uninvited guest to get from in front of our table. The waitress, whose name was Joy, looked nervous and begun to stutter when she asked if I was serious. When I stood up, she saw just how serious I was when I punched Nailah dead in her face. I saw her two friends rushing over, so I got into a fighting stance because I was prepared to fight all three of those bitches. Well, two bitches because Nailah was trying to stop her nose from leaking. By this time, the manager had intervened, telling Liem and I that we had to leave. I didn't give a flying fuck; I got to punch that bitch in the face and got a free meal - I was good. I thought Liem would be upset, but he cracked jokes all the way home. He said that I was in the wrong profession, and I could've been the next Hilary Swank from the movie, *Million Dollar Baby*. His ass is a whole fool; I had to remind him that it was just a movie, just like my punch was just a punch.

"Are we going to my place or am I taking you home?" he asked, still laughing.

"I'm going to go on home because Nailah got me in a crazy mood right now, and I have a paper to hand in tomorrow anyway," I said.

"Okay, I guess we'll have to pick this up another night, slugger," he laughed.

"I take it you're never going to let me live this down."

"I'm just messing with you, but from now on, you're going to be my little slugger."

"I don't want you thinking that I just go around punching people because I'm not that person. She provoked me," I said, wanting him to understand that I'm not that girl.

"I know that and don't take my jokes seriously because you really had no choice in the matter. I have no idea what her beef is," he said.

"That's just a female for you; they only want you when you stop chasing them and move on."

"I chased her for a very long time, so she can kick rocks for all I care," he said.

"Kick rocks? Your ass is crazy for chasing her ass anyway because everyone and their mama knows that she's nothing but a trick," I said.

"That's true, but you know most of the times men are thinking with the wrong head."

"Well, I just hope you got thinking with the wrong head out of your system," I said seriously.

"You don't have to worry about that; something about not knowing if you're going to live or die gives you a different perspective on life and how you want to live it."

I didn't even know that we were at my house already. I kissed him goodnight and got out of the car with a smile on my face because I still had the chance to give him a kiss on his soft lips. When I got inside, I put my book bag down and went to find my mother to see how her day went. I was hoping it went better than mine did. She was in her room and already sleeping; I couldn't wait until I was able to tell her that she didn't have to work anymore. I heard my phone ringing, and my face lit up. I knew it was Chink because *Best Friend* was her ringtone.

"What's up stranger? How are you?" I joked.

"I'm good, girl. Sorry I've been MIA, but I want to make it up to you. My stylist, Cyn, is having a party tomorrow night, and she invited me, so I'm inviting you," she said.

"Wait. Before I say yes or no, guess what?"

"Come on, Polo. We're how old? Just tell me," she laughed.

"Why can't you just go with the flow? Anyway, guess who has a man?"

"OMG! You and Liem? Yes, finally! It took you guys forever," she screamed.

"We've only known each other for a few months, girl, and I pray we aren't moving too fast."

"You two are cute together. I think you made a good choice, and correction, we have known Liem since high school."

"True, I just hope I made the right decision because I already had to punch Nailah's ass in the face over his ass. She had the nerve to try me, in a restaurant of all places. I tried to hold it together, because you know how I get down, but she took me there."

"Please say it didn't happen. Damn, Liem got to see the fighter in you already. What did he say?"

"His ass thought it was comical; he joked about it all the way to my house."

"So why was she flexing on you?"

"You know she always hated on us. I guess she and Liem had something before, and she was in her feelings seeing him with me, the white girl."

"Girl, your ass is blacker than anyone I know. Her ass will think twice about sleeping on your ass next time."

"These bitches be tripping. Anyway, what's been going on with you?" I asked her.

"Karen and I have been getting to know each other. I'm not going to lie; we have so much in common that there's no denying that she birthed me."

"Wow, so how do you feel about the whole being snatched ordeal with your grandmother?"

"At first I was upset with my mom, I mean my grandmother, but she's not here to defend herself. I have since forgiven her, and she's still my mom because she's the only mother I've ever known."

"Shit, I wouldn't have known how to feel, but I'm glad that you got the chance to meet your birth mother."

"I feel the same way. Now back to you; are you going with me to this party tomorrow night?"

"I guess I can hang with my best friend that I've been missing."

"The feeling is mutual. Love you, sis, and I will see you tomorrow night."

"Love you too; see you tomorrow," I said, ending the call.

I saw that Liem texted me to let me know that he made it home. I texted back, letting him know that I would try to call him after my homework, but it never happened because after it all was said and done, I got out of the shower and went straight to bed. I was out for the night.

CHAPTER FIFTEEN
CHINK

Cyn's man must have been making some serious paper. I really expected some ratchet, bullshit party, but this club was on point. Polo and I made our way over to the VIP. She could have stayed her ass at home because she hasn't stopped texting Liem since I met up with her ass. The waitress was here to take our drink orders, and she hadn't come up for air. I had to nudge her to get her attention.

"Polo, this is supposed to be me and you hanging out, away from Liem and Lah," I laughed.

"I'm sorry, girl. I don't know what it is about him; I just can't get enough of him," she said, smiling like a little schoolgirl.

"I understand, but damn, take a breather and give your girl some attention," I said, pouting as if I was upset, but I wasn't. I totally understood what she was feeling; it was that same feeling I had for Lah when I first started kicking it with him.

We were finally having a good time, getting our drink on. We were dancing with these two dudes that neither of us wanted to be dancing with; they rudely invited themselves. I looked at Polo, she looked at me, and we both walked off the dance floor, laughing our asses off. If dude thought he was going to be grinding all up on my ass and not even offer me a drink, he was wrong - not this girl. We walked back over to VIP, and Cyn finally showed up. I saw her walking towards us.

"Hey, Chink. I'm so glad you made it out; this is my better half, Drone, and his friend, Derek," she said.

I introduced them to Polo, who was back texting on her phone. She didn't even look up; she just gave them the head nod. I laughed to myself as I looked at Cyn's man and his friend. Drone looked like Pinky from the movie, *Friday After Next,* with his drip-drop top that he was sporting. That wet curl went out of style many, many years ago. His friend looked like Jerome from *Martin*; this scene was just fucking comical. Drone had to be banking because I couldn't see any other reason that would make Cyn deal with this dude.

"Hey, ladies. Are you enjoying yourselves?" some dude that I hadn't noticed until now asked.

Polo looked at me like, 'Is this dude serious?' One thing that I will say is that Drone's crew was some wannabe thugs. Polo ignored the dude and continued on her phone, so I had to deal with this clown.

"Yes, we're having a good time, just trying to enjoy the music," I said, hoping he got the message.

He didn't get the message as he sat down and talked my ear off about shit I wasn't interested in listening to. Polo thought the shit was funny, but I didn't find shit funny about it. I saw Cyn walking back over, and I was relieved when she told him to leave me alone because I had a man. He had the nerve to tell her to stop blocking as if he really had a chance with me. Niggas are so fucking thirsty; that's why I try to avoid the club scene. I pulled Polo up to walk with me to the ladies room because those drinks that I had were begging to be released right now.

On the way back from the bathroom, some tall, amazon looking chick bumped me. At first, I was going to let it slide because it was crowded. As I continued walking behind Polo, the bitch bumped me again, and that's when I knew it wasn't an accident. The bitch was doing it on purpose.

"What's the fucking problem?" I asked her.

Polo stopped walking and turned around, ready to get it popping. I wanted to laugh so badly because I swear when I stopped there were two or three people behind her, but her ass is always on point.

"Chink, who the fuck is this bitch?" she asked me.

I wanted to tell her to fall back and that I had this, but she has always been my protector, coming to my rescue since high school. It didn't matter that we were now adults; she never stopped feeling the need to protect me.

"Polo, I don't know who she is. She bumped me twice for no reason, and I'm trying to figure out what's the fucking problem," I answered, getting pissed.

"No, bitch, there is a reason, and if I see you in my man's face again, I'm going to fuck you up," she said.

"Bitch, what the fuck are you talking about? I have my own fucking man, and I damn sure don't need yours."

"So, you weren't just all up in my man's face, bitch?" she asked with spittle flying.

"If you're talking about that busted nigga that was just trying to holla at my girl, bitch, please," Polo said.

"If he was so busted, why the fuck was she sitting there, grinning and shit?" she said, looking dumb as shit.

"I can't with these bitches. Yo, why you got an attitude? Girl, that's everybody's dude cause your nigga ain't loyal," Polo sang, mocking K. Michelle's *Loyal* remix.

Everybody within earshot was laughing, and even her girls chuckled. The bitch got mad and stole on me. It was on as Polo went at that bitch; I was fighting one of her friends when another one jumped in. I was holding my own until a third bitch came out of nowhere. I was being kicked and punched all over my body. I grabbed one of those bitches by their hair and pulled her down as I saw Cyn and her girls jump in the fight. It was now even, and it was time for me to whip a bitch's ass, I flipped her over, got on top of her, and started beating the shit out of her. Just as I was about to start banging her head into the floor, I was grabbed from behind. I turned around to start swinging on whoever grabbed me, but I came face to face with Lah.

"Yo, calm the fuck down. Why you up in here fighting like a fucking hood rat?" he barked.

I'd never seen him this mad before. I didn't even get the chance to respond because Lah had to assist Liem, who was having a hard time holding Polo. When she goes from zero to one hundred, it's a wrap; she's gone. She was now swinging on both of them, and she only stopped when I called her name. Security was escorting big doofy and her friends out of the club. I couldn't believe that I just had a fight over some nigga that wasn't even mine. I had no kind of interest in that dude; this shit is crazy how these bird bitches always want to fight a female over their cheating ass men.

LAH

I was sitting on the couch at Chink's house watching television and drinking rum straight. I haven't said anything to her since we got back to the house. I wasn't upset with her, I was upset at the situation. I was chilling with Liem when he told me that Chink and Polo were at some club in Flushing. I wasn't bothered because I knew she was going out. What bothered me was the last text he got from Polo, telling him about Chink's friend's boyfriend, Drone, was being a cornball. He jumped up, knowing it was the same Drone that got his ass caught up. I knew it was the same Drone too because there weren't too many men with that name from Queens. I had to get Chink out of there before his punk ass decided to fuck up my world with his snitching ass. When I walked into the club, I wasn't expecting her and Polo to be in the club fighting. Polo was a handful, and I don't know if Liem was going to be able to handle little mama. I continued to sit in deep thought, letting my mind take me back to the day that might come back and haunt me, jeopardizing my relationship with Chink.

***

I was sitting in Drone's truck, waiting for him to end his call, so that we could handle business. He usually had us meet up at his bar over on the Van Wyck, but instead, tonight we met up at the water near the FDR.

"What's up, young blood?" he asked after he ended his call.

"Just chilling. I'm trying to get this money, so what do you need?" I asked him.

"This job is personal, and I'm willing to pay double for this job," he said.

"What's the job?" I asked, feeling like he was beating around the bush.

"I need for you to handle Rita that lives over on 115th Avenue," he said.

"What reason could you possibly have to want Ms. Rita killed?" I asked because she was a nice lady who never bothered anyone.

"Just know that I have history with her, and she took something that was my heart from me, so she has to pay."

He didn't give enough information for me to kill Ms. Rita. She was always cool people, even when she was kicking us from off of her porch. He sensed my hesitation and tripled the amount being offered. Reality set in that this was a job, and there was no time for feelings to be involved. It was business as usual as I agreed to do the job.

I remember the day as if it was yesterday because her face still haunts me in my dreams. When I knocked on her door she must have been expecting someone else because she yelled, "I told you hell no," when she opened up the door. When she saw that it was me standing there, looking puzzled, she said, "If you're here for my daughter, she isn't home. She's not allowed to date, so I need you to leave my porch and not return." She was never this unpleasant, so I took it as her being angry with whoever she expected to be at her door. I put my game face on and did what I did best.

"Ms. Rita, I'm not here for your daughter, and I'm not trying to date her or anything like that, but I do need to speak to you about her," I said.

"What would you possibly have to talk to me about concerning my daughter?" she asked.

"Your daughter goes to the same high school that my brother goes to, and he told me that he noticed that a man was at the school on two different days, just watching her," I lied.

"Oh my God!" she said, inviting me in.

I didn't think it would play out, but she looked shook and wanted me to give her a description of the man. Being that Drone mentioned that they had history, I decided to give his description to her. She ran up the stairs in a panic, and at first, I stood in the living room, stuck on stupid, as I wondered what just happened. After a few minutes, I decided to climb the stairs to see why she rushed off, leaving a complete stranger standing in her living room. Sure, she knew me from sometimes sitting on her porch, but she didn't know me well enough to leave me in her home unattended - even though it worked in my favor. Once I reached the top of the stairs, I heard her on the phone telling someone that he found her. I didn't want to waste any more time than I already had; now that she was on the phone that could mean that someone was on their way. I walked up behind her without notice, stabbing her numerous times. I like to shoot my victims, but Drone insisted that she be stabbed repeatedly until she stopped moving and was no longer breathing. I hightailed out of there. I already regretting taking her life, but it was too late; it was already done. I had no idea that years later I would be hooking up with her daughter.

"You still mad at me?" Chink asked, bringing me back to the present.

"I'm not mad at you; I just didn't expect you to be fighting in a club."

"I didn't expect to be fighting in the club either, but this chick came at me sideways over some dude that was all up in my face. He was trying to kick it like his girl wasn't at the club. So you see, I didn't initiate the fight, and I even told dude to step because I had a man," she said.

"You should have just walked away, not stoop to her level."

"I tried walking away after she bumped me the first time, but she bumped me again and then swung on me, so Polo rushed her. It was on from there."

"Yo, little mama is a beast. I would have never believed that she got down like that if I hadn't seen it with my own eyes," I laughed.

"Nobody really knows that she goes from zero to one hundred like that. She is the sweetest thing, but don't sleep on her," she said, laughing too.

"Trust me, I know that now. You saw how she flipped on me and Liem's ass."

"She didn't mean to flip on you or Liem. Her ass blacked out; she did apologize though," she said, still laughing.

160

"So since you said that you're not mad at me, how about you give me a massage? My body is killing me," she said, moaning as if she was in pain.

"You shouldn't have been fighting," I said as I began to give her a full body massage while she lay on the couch.

We both were quiet as she closed her eyes, enjoying her massage. I thought back to what needed to be done with Drone's ass. When I was leaving the club, he had the nerve to wink at me. I will not have a nigga holding anything over my head; his ass had to go.

"Do you want to order something to eat since we didn't stop to get anything to eat?" she asked.

"It's like midnight now. After this massage you better go in the kitchen and make us something to eat," I said seriously.

We ended up eating ham and cheese sandwiches and watching *Everybody Loves Raymond* until she dozed off. I couldn't sleep because I had murder on my mind. Chink had to be at the salon today. Once she leaves at eleven, I was going to go home. I needed some quiet time to figure out exactly how I wanted to end Drone's fucking life.

I sat in an old rusty Honda a few blocks from Drone's house, waiting for him to arrive home. His punk ass had no idea that I knew where he laid his head. It was getting late, and I told Chink that I would be there hours ago. This fuck nigga never came home; I should have had a better game plan. For all I knew, he could have been inside laid up with some bitch or not even home at all. 'That's alright,' I thought as I pulled off. I would make sure to be ready with a bulletproof plan the next time.

CHAPTER SIXTEEN
POLO

This was the second time Liem saw me in rare form, and again, he didn't judge me. He was a little upset that he got a right hook to the face, but he still didn't judge me. He understood that I was a good friend that had Chink's back. I was now at home texting my man while watching my recorded show of *Grey's Anatomy.*

Liem: Are you coming through tonight?

Me: I know your mom has to be tired of me being there all the time.

Liem: Nope, she loves that you come over so much because you keep me out of the streets.

Me: I don't think she has to worry about that. I believe you're done with the streets.

Liem: That's real talk. Anyway, are you coming? I miss you.

Me: I miss you too. Come get me.

Liem: I'm on my way.

I put my phone down, running around like a little schoolgirl trying to find something to wear while listening to K. Michelle's song, *Hard To Do,* from her new album. The song has become my favorite because it's actually how I felt about Liem's ass. I miss him when I don't see him, and I have wet dreams thinking about putting this pretty thing on him while fucking him.

"He must be some kind of special," my mom said from my doorway, watching me.

"He is, Mom. I never thought that I could feel this way again after Steven," I said smiling like a little schoolgirl again. It was becoming something that I did a lot lately.

"Well, if he's so special, when are you going to introduce him to your mother?" she asked.

"Mom, do you remember Ms. Dawn's son, Liem? He went to school with me and Chink?"

"Not that hardheaded boy that always stayed in trouble and was always chasing behind those fast tail girls," she asked with her nose turned up.

"Mom, that was high school. He's not like that anymore. He's a grown man who is working and saving for his own place and a new car."

"Well, when can I meet him?" she asked.

"He's on his way to pick me up. Do you want to meet him now?"

"Yes, I will meet him now," she said, leaving my doorway.

I ran out to the living room and grabbed my phone.

Me: Liem, my mom wants to meet you. NOW!

Liem: I'm turning the car around and going back home. LOL.

Me: She's not that bad. She just wants to meet you. She remembers you as a hardheaded teenager - her words not mine.

Liem: I'm not worried, shorty. I'm on my way.

I didn't mention to my mom that Liem was shot a few months ago, so I hoped it didn't come up in conversation. I knew she would judge him and forbid me from seeing him. I went back to my room and nervously got dressed. When I was done, I walked back into the living room and noticed that my mom had her scarf off and her wrap was down. She had changed into some tight ass jeans and a fitted tee. I looked at her like, why? 'Shit, he's not coming to see her,' I thought as I sat on the couch. I was wishing that he would hurry up so that we could get this introduction over with.

Liem rang the doorbell fifteen minutes later, walking in looking good enough to eat. He was dressed simply; he had on a fitted NY cap, bubble jacket, gray sweatpants, and some J's. He was killing that thug swag that I loved so much. He sat down on the sofa next to me. Mind you, it's a loveseat for two people, but my mom was acting like a teenager with a crush as she squeezed in between us, focusing on Liem.

"Mom, this is Liem. Liem, this is my mom, Pat," I said.

"Nice to meet you, Liem," she said with her hand on his knee.

I could tell that Liem was uncomfortable, so I stood up, ready to go. I didn't know what had gotten into my mom because I have never seen her act so flirtatious. She never acted this way with Steven, so I honestly didn't know what this was about.

"Mom, we are about to head out so we can get to the movie theater on time," I lied.

"Okay, baby, and Liem, don't be a stranger," she said, hugging him.

Once in the car, Liem and I looked at each other, and we both burst out laughing.

"Don't even ask. I have no idea what that was about," I said.

"That shit was awkward as hell," he laughed.

Liem drove to the Walmart in Green Acres; we picked up a DiGiorno pizza and boneless chicken combo for our movie night at his house. On the way out, we stopped at Red Box and got *Identity Theft* and *The Internship*. I kissed Liem's mom on the cheek and said hello to Cari before heading to his room. After we finished eating, we cuddled on the bed to watch the movies. I sat between his legs, resting my head on his chest. I wouldn't dare disrespect his mom by having sex in her house, but the way I was feeling right now, his ass could definitely get it. He didn't make it any better by kissing me on my neck and massaging the inside of my thigh. I shifted my body until I was facing him, and I closed my eyes as our lips touched. I felt his tongue in my mouth, and I sucked on it as if it was a good piece of candy. My panties got wet, and I had to break the kiss.

"Liem, I can't do this in your mother's house," I said, breathing heavy.

"I can lock the door; she's not going to know," he said, looking in my eyes.

I wanted so badly to tell him no, but who was I to deny this fine specimen in front of me? My body was betraying me as I said okay. He got up to lock the door.

"Liem, put some music on; I need something to calm my nerves," I said.

"Okay, let me see if I have some hip moving music," he said, laughing.

"Well, you better have some August Alsina or some K. Michelle."

He connected his phone to a speaker and got back on the bed as some reggae mix began to play from his phone's playlist.

I was still a little shook that we were in his mother's house, but I went with the flow as he unbuttoned my blouse. I'll be the first to admit that I'm far from being a virgin, but when he removed my bra, I felt like one as my body shivered. His big, juicy lips brushed against my right breast before he took it in his mouth. He was slow grinding on top of me as his body moved to the music. I got so into the feeling that I took over; I helped him pull his shirt over his head. He pulled my pants and panties off, and I helped him out of his sweatpants. I looked at his body, and I must say that he was working with a monster down there.

I told him to lie on his back because I wanted to ride. Even though I was a little scared, I had to ride it; it was calling my name. I kissed him as I climbed on top, and we got lost in the kiss until I couldn't take it anymore. I broke the kiss and whispered in his ear to get a condom because I was ready to feel the dick. I put the condom on and helped him enter me; he let out a low moan. I rode the tip of his dick first as I eased him inside of me; I had to hold my breath as it was taken away when all of him was inside of me. I don't know what happened, but when that next track came on, I started doing the Dutty Wine on his dick; it was a well-known Jamaican dance. He moaned loudly this time, and I had to tell him to be quiet. I was not trying to let his mom know that we were fucking. I got lost in the music as I tightened my pussy muscles and continued riding his dick with my hand over his mouth.

I guess he got tired of his eyes rolling into the back of his head and moaning like a little bitch because he flipped me on my stomach. He lifted my ass as he entered me, pounding in and out of me as if he had something to prove. I laughed to myself because men and their egos were too much. He was fucking my insides right as I backed my ass up. We fucked until neither of us had any more energy to bust another nut. I lay in his arms, thinking, 'I've never been fucked like he just fucked me,' as I dozed off.

I woke up and realized that I had stayed out all night. Liem's mom and Cari had already left for church. I knew my mother was probably at work already. I wasn't worried about her flipping; she's probably more worried than anything else because I've never stayed out overnight unless I was spending the night with Chink. I grabbed my phone out of my bag. I had a few missed calls from her and a text message, asking me to give her a call. I texted her back, letting her knows that I was okay. I told her that I was on my way home and would see her when she got off work. I woke Liem up to tell him that I needed to get home.

LIEM

I just dropped Polo off at her crib, and my ass was missing her already. I opted out of staying for a while because as much as I missed her, I didn't want to run into her mom again. I know Polo didn't know that her mom was an undercover cougar; her ass was fucking with my boy, Tre. The first time I met her mother was at Tre's crib. Like I said, she fucking with him, but she was pressing up on me hard - right in front of my boy. He didn't have a problem with it, so me being young and chasing pussy, I bent her ass over the couch and fucked the shit out of her. In my defense, I had no idea that she was Polo's mother until I walked in her crib yesterday. My first year in high school I'd seen her mother maybe once or twice, and she was a little on the heavy side - nothing like she looks now. I don't know if I should have said something to Polo or not, but if she was to find out, I hope she doesn't hold it against me. We weren't together, and I had no idea she was her mother. The way her mother was acting when she saw me, I knew that she remembered me.

I called Lah up to see what he was up to. We agreed to meet up for drinks, so I was headed his way. I know what you're thinking, 'Having drinks on a Sunday?' Yes, it's Sunday, but I needed a damn drink, and I needed to holla at my big brother about this situation. When I arrived at Rawlins Bar & Grill, Lah was already seated.

"What's up, bro?" I asked him because his ass looked how I was feeling.

"I can't call it. What's going on with you?"

"Do you remember my boy, Tre, that I went to school with? The one that I was always getting in trouble with?"

"Yeah, I remember him. What's up with his ass?" he asked.

"I haven't spoken to him since all this shit happened, but the last time I was at his crib, he was telling me about some older chick that he was kicking it with. He said she was a straight freak. She came through while I was there, pressing me real hard for the dick. Tre gave me that 'ain't no fun if the homeys can't have none' look, so I fucked the bitch."

"Nigga, you wild for that shit," he laughed.

"Nah, that's not even the wild part. It turns out that the older bitch was Polo's mom," I said, shaking my head.

"Stop fucking lying," he said, still laughing.

"I kid you not. Polo hit me up telling me that she wanted me to come inside when I picked her up because her mother wanted to meet me. As soon as I got in the crib, I recognized her. She started flirting, touching my knee and shit right in front of Polo."

"Say word, my nigga."

"Word. I played that shit off, but now I don't know if I should tell shorty or let that shit rock. To be honest, I think her mom is going to be a problem."

"Damn, nigga. I wish my problem was that simple, but my advice to you is to just let that shit rock," he said.

"Now on to your ass. What's got you so stressed out?" I asked him.

"I didn't tell you this shit, but I used to work for Drone," he blurted out.

"Fuck you mean you used to work for Drone? You gave me that bullshit speech, and your ass was working for him too?" I said, not caring that I interrupted his ass.

"Don't get shit twisted. I wasn't out here nickeling and diming for no nigga. I was being paid to lay niggas down," he said.

I sat in shock because I had no idea that my brother was on some murder-one shit. I just looked on in complete silence as I let him continue.

"So a few years ago, Drone came to me about a personal hit. He wanted me to hit Ms. Rita, and I hesitated at first because she was always a nice lady. When he tripled the payment though, I agreed to do it. As you know, Ms. Rita was Chink's mom, but I had no idea that Chink and I would get together on any level. Now I have the same question for you. Do you think that I should just come clean and tell her? Keep in mind that Drone's punk ass is threatening to tell her because after I found out that he had you on payroll, I fucked his ass up."

I thought about everything that he just said, trying to digest it all, and my problem didn't seem like much of a problem anymore. I honestly didn't think he should come clean because how could you tell someone that you killed their mother and think that shit would be forgiven? His ass is fucked. Unless...

"I say we body that nigga. I still feel like he had something to do with me getting hit, so I say we hit his ass."

"That's what I'm talking about my nigga; we have to figure out how we're going to do this shit though," he said, getting hyped.

We knocked back a few more drinks before going our separate ways - after coming up with a bulletproof plan to take Drone's punk ass out.

CHAPTER SEVENTEEN
POLO

I was sitting on my bed Indian style, doing my homework, when my mother walked in. She looked like she had something on her mind. I looked away from my homework and gave her my attention to see what she wanted.

"Hey, baby. Do you have a few minutes? I need to talk to you?" she asked.

"I'm just finishing up. Give me ten minutes, and I'll meet you in the living room," I told her.

I knew that if I got up now, I wouldn't want to finish. I was working on this case scenario assignment that was given in my criminology class. I had to choose to be the prosecutor or the defense on this case study. I decided to be the prosecutor, so my opening statement was due on Tuesday, and my closing argument was due by the end of the same week. To be honest, I really didn't have time to take a break to chat it up with my mother. After finishing my closing argument, I went into the living room to see what my mother wanted to talk to me about. She was sitting on the couch, watching the news.

"Hey, Mom. What did you need to talk to me about?" I asked her.

"I wanted to talk to you about Liem," she said, lowering the sound on the television.

"What about him?" I asked, already getting defensive.

"I just think that you can do better, and you shouldn't be wasting your time with him."

"That's funny, coming from you, because I couldn't tell that you didn't like him."

"I didn't say that I didn't like him. I said that you can do better and shouldn't be wasting your time."

"Mom, what would be better? Would it be a man who is twice my age and cheating on me? You didn't have a problem with me dating an older man - when you should have. So what's the problem with me dating Liem?"

I didn't mean to take that tone with her, but she was pissing me off by being a fucking hypocrite. She was all giddy with Liem; now all of a sudden, she doesn't want me to see him anymore. 'Get the fuck out here,' I thought as I just looked at her ass.

"Patricia, don't forget that I'm your mother, and you will respect me as such," she said.

"I'm not trying to disrespect you; I just don't understand the problem you have with Liem."

176

"Do you really want to know what my problem is with your little boyfriend?" she asked.

"I wouldn't have asked if I didn't want to know," I said, getting sick of the conversation.

"There you go with that smart ass mouth again. I'm seconds from punching you in it," she spat.

Tears started stinging my eyes, threatening to fall, because my relationship with my mother has always been a good one. She was my best friend; I could talk to her about anything and vice versa, so for her to be coming at me like this was hurtful and not like her. I looked up at her with hurt in my eyes as she continued being the complete opposite of who she has always been to me.

"You can wipe those fucking tears; I'm just trying to save you from being heartbroken by him later. So it's best that you learn the truth about him now, and who better to tell you the truth than your mother?"

"Mom, what truth are you talking about? What are you not saying?" I asked, getting pissed off again.

"Did your little boyfriend tell you that he slept with your mother?" she said, lighting a cigarette.

"What are you talking about he slept with you? When? Where? How?" I ranted off each question; I was

177

totally confused at this point as to what she was talking about.

Now she wanted to just sit there saying nothing and blowing smoke in my direction. I felt like picking up something and bashing her fucking head in, but I took a few breaths before speaking again.

"So Mom, are you going to tell me when you slept with Liem?" I asked, voice cracking.

"Patricia, I'm not trying to hurt you. Like I said, I'm trying to help you. He's no different from any other man. He walked in this house, knowing that he had slept with your mother, and said nothing. A real man would have told you," she said, getting angry and sounding like a scorned ex-girlfriend.

My heart was hurting right about now. All I wanted was answers, but she just kept going around the questions. I felt a burning inside that was begging to be released, so out of fear of hurting my mother, I grabbed my coat, book bag, and cell phone and left the house. I stood on the porch in the cold and called Latch Car Service to come and pick me up to take me to Chink's house. I thought about calling Liem but dismissed that thought as fast as it came.

CHINK

The shop was really busy today, and I was so happy that the end was nearing. Cyn walked around giving me the cold shoulder all day. I was busy, so I really didn't have time to address what her problem was. After the last customer left out of the shop, I went over to her station to finally get to the bottom of why she has been giving me shade all day. It wasn't that I cared, but I'll be damned if she was going to be up in my shop acting as if I worked for her ass.

"Okay, Cyn. It's just you and me now, so do you want to tell me what the attitude is about?"

"I don't have an attitude. I'm just in my feelings. Is that a crime?" she asked.

"No, it's not a crime, but it's not a good look for business with you walking around giving me the cold shoulder all day - especially since it's towards your boss."

"My boss? That's funny," she laughed, being sarcastic.

"So, I'm not your boss?" I asked her.

"No, you're not my boss. You're a shop owner who I pay to work a station to serve my clientele," she said.

"I'll give you that, but it still boils down to the fact that I'm the owner of this shop. My shop will run how I

179

see fit, including you not walking around with a fucking attitude and not being woman enough to say what the fucking problem is," I said, pissed the fuck off.

"Trust, I'm all woman, but can you say the same? You walk in here and offer no apology. Instead, you walk around like shit is all good," she had the nerve to say.

"What reason do I owe you a fucking apology?" I asked, not caring that I was getting loud.

"You owe me an apology because you and your home girl came to my man's club, acting all ratchet. My girls and I had to act just as ratchet, coming to rescue your asses from getting fucked up. Now, my man is upset with me over your bullshit, but you don't owe me an apology, right? Okay."

This bitch must have fell and bumped her fucking head. I wish I would apologize for some shit I didn't start. If anything, she should be apologizing to my ass. Her man's friend was the one all up in my face, knowing his bitch was in the club, so he started all this bullshit.

"Well, if it makes you feel any better, my man was mad at me too, so get the fuck over it already," I said.

"Really, that's how you feel? I have always had respect for you, but I see you're no fucking different from these other bitches."

"Cyn, you're the fucking one coming at me sideways. Your fucking pimp of a man is mad at you, so you feel like you have the right to come in my shop, acting like a fucking bitch all day. And now, you're trying to insult me. Get your life, bitch."

"Bitch, I know you don't want to talk about my man; he may look like a pimp, but at least my man has a fat motherfucking bank account to go with it. And since you're on the subject of men, you need to know that yours isn't a saint."

"Well, if he has so much fucking money, get him to buy you a fucking shop. Your services are no longer needed here," I said.

I was done with the back and forth; this bitch needed to leave my shop and leave now - before I put my foot in her fucking ass. Talking about my man wasn't a fucking saint like she knows my fucking man. Bitch, bye.

"That's fine because I don't need you or your fucking shop," she said, packing her station up.

"And I don't fucking need you either," I yelled.

"Make sure you remember that when that snake of a fucking man breaks your fucking heart, bitch," she said.

"Cyn, I'm not going to be too many more bitches, and miss me with all the talk about my man because you don't know shit about my man," I said.

"See, that's where you're wrong. My old pimp of a man loves to pillow talk, and I know an earful about your man. Sweetie, you're sleeping with the enemy."

"Fuck you and fuck your man. Like I said, you don't know shit about my man," I said, just a little shaken by what she said.

"Correction. I didn't know shit about your man, but what I do know now is that your man worked for my man - just like his punk ass brother did. When your man found out that his brother got shot and was working for Drone, he came and violated, so my man came home pissed off. I sexed him to relieve some of his stress, and that's when he told me that Lah was responsible for killing your mother. Once he realized that he said too much, he threatened me that the information better not leave his bedroom. It didn't until now because it's always a slick talking bitch that you have to knock off of their high horse," she said, walking out of the salon door.

I wanted to follow her and hit her ass over the head until she admitted that she was lying, but I couldn't breathe. It felt like someone knocked the wind out of me. I didn't have asthma, but it sure felt like I was having an attack. I picked up the phone to call Polo, but it went straight to her voicemail, so I called Karen, barely able to speak. I managed to ask her to come to the shop to get me, and she said that she was on her way. When Karen walked in, I was sitting on the floor with my head on my knees, rocking back and forth.

"Chink, what happened?" she asked, helping me up off the floor.

"Please, just take me home," I said, just above a whisper.

I didn't want to talk about it; I just wanted to go home. When we walked in my house, Polo was sitting on the couch, Indian style with red eyes. I could see the hurt in her eyes, and I'm sure she saw the hurt in my eyes too. I didn't know what happened with her, but I do know that we both were happy a few hours ago. Karen's motherly instinct naturally kicked in naturally as she did her best trying to comfort us. She knew that I wasn't ready to talk, so she tried to get Polo to tell her what happened with her.

"Polo, sweetie, do you want to talk about what has you so upset?" she asked, rubbing her back.

Polo removed her legs from up under her and took a deep breath before attempting to tell us what happened and why it had her so upset.

"I was in my room doing my homework when my mom asked if she could speak to me. She said that she didn't think that Liem was the right man for me, and I should leave him alone. I asked her why, and she told me that she had slept with him," she cried, getting choked up.

Karen gasped. I cried out for the pain my friend was in, but at the same time, I wished that Lah had just slept with someone else because that, I could move on from. I got up and hugged my friend through my pain.

"I asked her to tell me when she slept with him, but she continued to act like a scorned girlfriend," she said, just above a whisper.

"Do you believe her?" I asked her because I couldn't see Liem sleeping with her mom.

"I don't know what to believe because like I said, she started acting like a scorned ex-girlfriend who was trying to hurt the new girlfriend," she said.

"Did you speak to Liem about what she said?" I asked her.

"No, I'm not ready to talk to him. Not while I'm still upset," she said, wiping her eyes.

I told them what was bothering me after a few hours. Yes, that's how long it took me to even want to repeat what Cyn said to me, but I did. It didn't make me feel any better after telling them what she said because Karen told me what my mom told her a few hours before she was killed. I felt sick to my stomach; Lah has been calling, and he even came by the house. Karen asked him to leave, but not before he asked her why I didn't want to see him. I wasn't ready to ask him or hear his explanation right now.

Polo decided that she wanted an explanation from Liem, so she was meeting up with him. I think she was doing the right thing. Being she couldn't get an explanation from her mother, who better to get one from? My phone chirped, letting me know I had another text message. I knew it was Lah without even looking at it.

Lah: Chink, please pick up the phone and call me and let me know why you're not speaking to me. It's only fair to tell me what I did before you just convict me. Hit me back.

The nerve of his ass. He knows, just like I know, that there would only be one reason why I would stop speaking to him. I sat on my bed with my tears falling, letting K. Michelle's song, *Bury My Heart,* sing the words that described exactly how I felt in that moment. I didn't understand why I wasn't as mad at him as I should have been. Instead, a piece of me wished that he was here to hold me in his arms and make the pain go away, but how can the man that broke my heart be the man that I'm yearning for? It took everything in me not to text him back or pick up the phone to tell him to come over because I needed him.

Karen left about an hour ago because she had to be to work early tomorrow morning. She had a meeting that she wasn't able to miss or else she said that she would have stayed the night with me. Polo said that she was coming back to stay the night, but I haven't heard from her yet, so I guess that her and Liem were working out what her mother told her.

I got up to go to my Mom's room, trying to find comfort in her bed, but feeling her presence didn't make me feel any better. The tears of guilt for sleeping with the man that may have been responsible for her not being here any longer seeped in. Anger started to take over after I realized that Cyn could have said something to me way before now because then my heart wouldn't have been involved, and I wouldn't have given my virginity to him. She wasn't my best friend, but I did consider her a friend who has been rocking with me and working at my shop for the past two years. She has only been with Drone for about eight months, and it's fucked up that her loyalty was with his ass.

My phone was ringing, and seeing that it was Lah again, I sent him to voicemail. He better believe that he will get his day, but today isn't that day, so he needs to just leave me alone. I picked up the phone to call Polo to see if everything worked out with her and Liem and to see if she was coming back to stay the night with me, but her phone went straight to voicemail. Her mom had the nerve to call and ask me if she was here, and I told her that I haven't seen her. I always liked her mom, but my loyalties lie with my best friend. After how her mother did her, with her approach of telling her about Liem, I was pissed off because no mother should ever knowingly hurt their child.

My eyes were getting very heavy, so I got up to take a shower in an attempt to allow the water to soothe me from the headache that I felt coming on. After my shower, I went back to my room, laid my head on my pillow, and dozed off with a heavy heart - wishing that I could really just bury my heart.

CHAPTER EIGHTEEN
LAH

Liem called me to let me know that Polo's mom told her about them sleeping together. Although he was upset with her mother, he said that he was glad that it was out because the stress of it was killing him. He also said that Polo was hurt because he should have told her instead of her finding out about it from her mom. I was happy for him that they were going to try and work it out, but when he confirmed what I already knew about why Chink stopped speaking to me, I was pissed. He said that Polo wanted my blood for hurting her friend, but he said that he convinced her that I didn't even know who Drone or the chick was that told Chick that bullshit story. I just didn't believe that his bitch ass dry-snitched on me to a bitch. I knew that I was going to stick with the original plan of putting Drone's ass six feet under, along with the bitch that repeated the shit to Chink.

If Chink gave me a chance to talk to her, I already made up my mind that I was going to tell her that Drone was lying and trying to get back at me for kicking his ass. I will convince her that he is responsible and even offer to avenge her mother's death. I know it sounds grimy, but

I'm willing to do whatever it takes because I'm not willing to lose her over a mistake that I made. My heart will never be the same if I were to lose her.

I was on my way to work, hoping that Karen would listen to me and help me by convincing Chink to hear me out. I stopped at Starbucks, located in the lobby of the hospital, to get her a coffee and a blueberry muffin as a peace offering to hear me out. I knew that if I could convince her at least to speak to Chink on my behalf, I had a fighting chance. I also knew that I had to put in everything I learned in that drama class I took in high school because I needed to bring my A-game with this act that I planned on putting on. Karen was sitting at her desk, signing into her computer. I walked up on her and handed her the coffee and the muffin. She didn't say anything as she took it from me, just giving me the side eye. I knew that I needed to speak before she sent me on my way.

"Karen, I know that you have to be in a meeting at nine thirty, so I'm not going to keep you. I was just wondering if we can have lunch today so that I can speak with you."

"Lah, you know that I like you. I always liked you even before I knew you were dating my daughter; you always seemed to have a good head on your shoulders, and I'm praying that what I heard isn't true. I will give you a chance to speak with me, but I also want you to keep in mind that whatever my daughter decides, I will support her."

"I understand, but I didn't do this. Thanks for agreeing to meet me for lunch to at least hear me out," I said, smiling on the inside.

"No problem, Lah," she said, taking a sip of her coffee.

I walked away with a huge smile on my face. I didn't even have to put my theatrical act in to play just yet. I honestly believe that Karen thought that I was telling the truth about not being involved in killing the woman that Chink believed to be her biological mother. I have a few work orders on my desk, so I figured that by the time I completed them, it would be time for lunch. I checked my work email before beginning, and I had an email from my mom, asking me to stop by her office sometime today. I felt bad for not spending much time with her, but my time was limited because I was spending all of my time at Chink's house, only coming home long enough to change clothes and then heading right back out. I made a mental note to stop by to see her later and set something up so that we could spend some time together.

When I got to the hospital cafeteria, Karen was already seated and waiting on me. I was nervous, but I put my game face on and kept it moving toward the table she was sitting at. She was wearing her game face too because I couldn't read her facial expression. I just hope that she kept in mind what she said about me earlier because it was true. I really did have a good head on my shoulders; I just made some mistakes along the way, but if Chink takes me back, I'm going to put all of that behind me and start off fresh.

"Karen, can I get you anything before I sit down?" I asked her, trying to break the ice.

"No, thank you. I just need to hear what you have to say. I have a lot of work on my desk from this morning because of the meetings, so I'm only taking a twenty minute lunch break today," she said.

I sat down, getting my thoughts together before speaking. All of that fly shit I was talking about bringing my A-game went out the back door because I was nervous and couldn't even remember what I wanted to say or how I wanted to say it. I knew that I had to say something before she got impatient and told me that she had to leave.

"Karen, Polo told my brother that some chick at Chink's job told her that her boyfriend, Drone, said that I was responsible for killing her mother. Karen, I have never had any contact with this Drone character on any level until I found out that he was the reason my brother was shot and left for dead. I went to his bar looking for him, and when I found him, I beat him down. That I will admit to, but anything else is a lie. I guess this is payback. Once he found out that I was dating Chink, he got his girlfriend to spin this story about me, and for him to be talking about the murder of Chink's mom, he has to be involved," I said, pretending to wipe a tear away.

"I do believe you. Only because just before Chink's mom died, she told me about the history she had with Drone. She said that he was looking for her to cause her harm, so I do believe that he found her and killed her, but Chick is who you need to convince," she said.

"Karen, Chink hasn't known me long, but she should know that I'm not capable of this. What kind of man does she believes me to be? Does she really think I'm capable of killing her mother and then having a relationship with her in the same house her mother was killed in? I would have to be a monster to do some shit like that," I said, pretending to get pissed off.

"What you're saying makes a lot of sense, but again, I'm not the one you need to convince."

"Karen, I'm not trying to convince you of anything; I'm just stating the facts. If you can talk to Chink and ask her to just hear me out, I will state the facts to her too."

"Lah, I will try and get her to have a sit down and talk with you about it, but I'm not making any promises that she will agree."

"Well, I need you to be as convincing when you ask her to hear me out as I was when I did it for you when you came knocking on her door."

She looked at me like, 'No, you didn't,' but yes, I did pull the guilt card because she owed me. Chink wasn't trying to give her the time of day when she came to her door, asking for her to just hear her out. If it wasn't for me, she would have sent Karen on her merry way, and they probably wouldn't have a relationship right now. She needed to talk to Chink and not stop talking until Chink said that she would hear me out.

After Karen said that she would talk to Chink and reach out to me later on that day, she got up to get back to work. I went over to get me a prepackaged club sandwich and a Sprite with a smile on my face. I felt it in my soul that Chink was going to agree to hear me out.

I was in such a better mood after speaking to Karen that I went to see my mother as soon as I finished lunch.

She was talking to the administrator, so I waited for her outside her office, talking to another co-worker until she was done. After about ten minutes, my mother was finishing up.

I walked into her office and took a seat. I haven't been to her office in a minute; I noticed that she had new furniture and a few new pictures. She also had pictures from the holiday party lined on her desk.

"Hello, son. I never thought that I would see the day that I would have to communicate with my child via email," she said sarcastically.

"Mom, it's not like that. I have just been busy, but I'm here now."

"So busy that you didn't have time to check on your mother? I heard about what happened to Dawn's son. I knew that boy was bad news," she said.

"Mom, he's not just Ms. Dawn's son, he's my brother. What happened to him wasn't his fault; he just happened to be in the wrong place at the wrong time," I lied.

"I don't believe in being in the wrong place at the wrong time; it has everything to do with the company you keep," she said.

"Mom, I know you didn't call me to your office to talk about my brother; I thought this was about you missing your son," I said, getting aggravated.

"I do miss you, Lahmiek. I was just pointing out that you have no time for your mother because if it's not that girlfriend of yours, it's your father's child taking all of your time from me."

"Mom, it's not like that, and if you're not busy this weekend, I would love to take you out to dinner so that we can catch up," I said.

"Are you sure your girlfriend isn't going to have a problem with you spending time with your mother?" She continued being sarcastic.

"She's not like that, Mom. You need to take some time and get to know her because she is going to be your daughter-in-law and the mother of your grandchildren," I said, speaking it into existence.

"Lahmiek, please tell me you didn't get this girl pregnant. You haven't even known her long enough to be speaking about marriage and babies," she said, holding her chest.

"No, she isn't pregnant, but she is going to be my wife in the near future, so I need for you to meet her and get to know her," I said.

I know I was misleading my mom into believing that everything was okay between Chink and I, but I was hoping that after she speaks to me, we can put it behind us and go back to the perfect relationship that we had before her friend destroyed it. I left my mother's office with her agreeing to go out to dinner with me on Sunday, but only after I agreed to go to church with her.

After work, I went straight home to wait and pray that Chink would be calling me to tell me to come by so that we could talk. My boy, Devin, wanted me to hang out with him at the after work spot. We frequented it at least twice a week to throw back drinks and to unwind after a hard workday, but I told him that I couldn't. My mind was on one thing and one thing only - getting my baby, Chink, back.

CHAPTER NINETEEN
CHINK

Today was not a good day, and everyone in the shop could feel it by the vibe I was giving off. If that wasn't a dead giveaway, my attire was. I had my braids pinned up in a messy bun, and I was wearing a sweat suit with sneakers. Anyone that knew me or frequented my shop knew that I always looked my best because I always felt that you have to represent yourself when running a business. If I didn't look good, how could I represent making someone else look good? The shop was overbooked today because instead of rescheduling Cyn's clients, I discussed helping out with the other stylists, and they agreed. I hated to reschedule when a client had an appointment because you never know what arrangements that person made to make that appointment or what function they may have to attend. I was wondering why Cyn didn't call her clients, knowing that she no longer worked at the shop; they have been showing up all week. I guess that man with the big bank account that she bragged about was accommodating her ass as she claimed he would.

I have been on edge most of the day because I agreed to meet up with Lah tonight at my house. Polo will be there with me for moral support; he was only getting a chance because Karen went to bat for him. She stated that she believed him, and she convinced me to hear him out. I have been having some doubts about him having anything to do with my mother's death as well because, after thinking about the whole situation with a clear mind, it all seemed coached on Cyn's part. When we spoke that same night after the club, she didn't have any issues with either Polo or me. She said that she was calling to check on us to make sure that we were okay, and she left it at that, so to come to the shop and flip the script was a little suspect to me.

"Chink? Girl, what's going on with you? And where the hell is Cyn?" Ciara, who is one of Cyn's regular clients, asked.

I really didn't feel like having this conversation because if I entertained it, she would never stop with the questions. I told her that Cyn had a family emergency to attend to this week. I thought that would get her off the subject, but it didn't.

"Well, that's not what I heard. I heard that you and Cyn had a falling out at the club because her boyfriend

198

was flirting with you, and it came to blows," she said. Ciara now had an audience waiting for my response.

"Ciara, I don't know where you heard that foolishness because that's far from the truth. That's what you should keep in mind before you speak. Everything that you hear isn't true, and you should think twice about repeating it," I said, getting aggravated.

Ciara has always been a shit starter who loved to keep shit going, but I wasn't in the mood for her ass today. If she knew any better, she would know to stop all that moving around with the theatrics before Dymond burned out the rest of her damaged baldhead. She comes to the shop faithfully every two weeks, which is good, but in between her visits she doesn't keep up her hairstyle by wrapping it, combing it, or washing it. Her hair was barely growing; in fact, it was falling out more, but it didn't stop her from coming to the shop every two weeks. I honestly believe that she comes to the shop to waste her money and start some shit. That's what bitches with no life do; they live for bullshit. I ignored Ciara and got back to concentrating on my client's hair because Ciara's ass was one step away from getting her ass kicked.

***

I walked around to the front of the building after leaving out the back door. I don't usually leave out the back door, but Dymond forgot to empty the trashcans inside the shop and take the garbage out back, so I had to do it. The cold wind blowing sent chills through my body as I rushed to get to my car. Just as I reached my car, I felt a presence behind me. My mind was telling me to run, but my body was frozen in place. After a few seconds, my body went into survival mode as I reached my hand into my pocket, pulling out the can of mace that I kept inside. I turned around to spray whoever it was standing behind me, but I wasn't quick enough. He knocked it out of my hand, pissing me off once I saw who it was.

"Drone, why are you here? Cyn no longer works here," I said.

"I'm not here to see Cyn; I came to see you," he answered.

"See me about what?" I said, getting pissed off.

"My girl told me that you were talking about me, and I find that to be very disrespectful, seeing as how I spared you your life."

"What the hell are you talking about you spared my life? I don't even know you, just like you don't know me."

"I know you, and you're right. You wouldn't know me because you were too young at the time, but I was the man who snatched you when you were just two years old. You also don't know that your family and I go way back. We have history," he said, smirking.

I was freaking out right about now because I needed to get away from his ass. I remember being snatched, and if he's claiming to be the person that snatched me, I knew that this wasn't a friendly visit. His ass was here to hurt me, but why now? My phone began ringing with Polo's ringtone, and I attempted to reach into my bag to answer it, but he knocked the bag out of my hand to the ground.

"Trust. By the time they come looking for you, it will be too late," he barked.

He grabbed me by my coat, forced my head down toward the ground where the bag fell, and told me to pick it up. After I had the bag in my hand, he told me to unlock the door to the shop. I started to tell him to kick rocks until I saw the gun that was now in his hand. My brave persona went out the window when I saw the gun. He had me send Polo a text message, telling her that I was running late. I knew that she wouldn't worry and come looking for me after reading my text, so that dashed my hope of someone coming to help me. He took the phone and threw it against the wall, cracking it to pieces.

"Now that we have that out of the way, let me continue. Like I said, I have history with your family. Rita and I were together since high school and continued to be together for years after we graduated. When Rita told me that she was pregnant with my child, she made me the happiest man alive. I loved Rita with everything that I had, and when my baby girl was born, I loved her just the same. When Rita found out that I was messing around with her best friend, she was hurt and refused to see me. I really didn't care that she didn't want to see me anymore. I was young, and new pussy was better than stressing over old pussy, but I missed my baby girl something crazy. I begged her to forgive me because at this point, I was willing to do anything to see my baby girl. She told me that I only cared about our daughter and not about her, so I would never see my daughter again. About a week later, I got the call that my daughter was killed in an accident. They said my daughter fell into the pool and drowned," he said, wiping at his tears that had fallen.

I felt sorry for him, but then again, none of this has anything to do with me. I wasn't even thought of when he and my mother met and his daughter died, and I was just a child when they went through their domestic abuse.

"I didn't care that the police ruled it an accident; I knew that Rita killed my daughter, so from that day forward, I made a vow to make her feel exactly how she made me feel when she took my daughter away from me. I recruited her son to work for me, drug trafficking out of state, without her knowing, and as soon as he was comfortable with his new position, I had him killed. I waited a little over a year after his death for her to mourn him and live miserably before I reconciled with her to gloat. I want to watch her in pain, but she was far from in pain. She now had another little girl, who was about six months old, and it triggered something in me. I abused her every day because I didn't think she should be happy and get to feel joy again when my heart had a hole in it from missing my daughter," he said, now getting angry all over again.

"I'm confused. What does all of this have to do with me? She's gone," I cried out.

I was so angry that the tears just fell because he just admitted to having my mother killed and my father, who I never had the chance to meet. This man has taken so much from me, and I have no idea what more he wanted from me. Why can't he just let me be? Doesn't he realize that I'm a victim in all that happened when I was a child?

"I can see that you're angry, but guess what? I'm angry too. And if you're wondering why I'm here, you can blame your boyfriend for this visit. I hope he didn't think that he could put hands on me and there would be no consequences."

"Again, what does that have to do with me? I had nothing to do with him putting hands on you. Why don't you take that shit up with him, man to man?"

"I will take it up with him, but I need to do something so that he can come to me. And when he does, his mom is going to need that black dress to bury both her sons," he said, now pointing the gun at me.

"Please, don't do this; I have nothing to do with…"

I didn't even get to finish my sentence as I felt the first bullet hit me in my shoulder. My hand reached up to touch the spot where I was shot, only to feel myself being hit two more times before falling to the floor. I closed my eyes until I heard him leave out of the back door. The burning in my chest was so intense, but I knew that I didn't want to die. I was losing blood and starting to feel lightheaded. I slid my body as close to the counter as I could, reached up, and tried to ignore the pain as I grabbed the cordless phone to call 911. That's the last thing I remembered before blacking out.

CHAPTER TWENTY

LAH

When Chink never showed up at home, Polo and I drove to the shop. We were worried because if she was going to be this late, she would have texted Polo again or even called. As soon as we pulled up to the shop, it looked like a crime scene on a television show. The yellow tape was blocking off the entrance of the shop, and a few officers were standing outside. After we told one of the officers that we were family of the owner of the shop, he informed us that Chink was shot and taken to Booth Memorial Hospital. I tried my best to hold it together for Polo because she was a mess. I needed to console her by telling her that Chink would be okay, but I wasn't so sure; I just hoped that she would be. When we got to the hospital, they told us that she was still in surgery and that someone would be out to speak to the family soon.

Just about all of her family arrived at the hospital, and there wasn't a dry eye in the waiting area. I was fuming that she was shot and left for dead. This shit had Drone written all over it, and I was mad at myself because I should have killed his ass way before now. I felt really bad for Polo; she was sitting in the corner, crying and staring off into space, and Liem was trying his best to console her. Karen was pacing back and forth, mumbling to herself, until the doctor came out of the double doors and asked for the family of Chasity Montgomery. I held my breath, waiting for the doctor to speak.

"I need for the family of Chasity to please follow me," he said, walking back through the double doors.

We all followed him to a private quarter of the hospital and into a room that looked more like a boardroom; it felt as if we were about to have a meeting. Once everyone was seated, we all waited for him to speak and update us on Chink's condition.

"My name is Dr. Wells, and I'm one of the doctors working to save Chasity's life. She came into the hospital with gunshot wounds to her shoulder, chest, and torso. The bullet in her shoulder entered and exited on its own. We were able to remove the bullet from her chest and repair the damage to her lung. She's still in surgery, but I stepped out because we have some concerns about the removal of the bullet to her torso. We need the family to tell us how you want us to proceed," he said, looking around the room to make sure everyone was following what he was requesting as he continued.

"Chasity lost a lot of blood, and she was given a blood transfusion. A sonogram was performed that let us know that she is eight weeks pregnant. If we attempt to remove the bullet from her torso, there is a possibility that the bullet may shift and harm the fetus," he said.

"Do whatever you have to do to save Chink. She can always have another baby, but we only have one of her," her Aunt Shirley said.

Everyone in the room was in agreement, but I was having a hard time agreeing with that decision. I didn't know that she was pregnant, but now that I do, I'd rather they try and save both of them.

"Doctor, I understand how the family is feeling, and they have every right to feel that way, but that's my girlfriend and child on that operating table. I want you to do everything that you need to do to bring both of them out of this alive," I said.

"Son, I don't know if you're serious right now, but we will not be risking my niece's life for an eight-week-old fetus that's not even acknowledged as a baby right now. Like my wife said, Chink can have more kids, so we all need to be focused on saving her life," her uncle said.

"With all due respect, it may only be an eight-week-old fetus, but it's a fetus that belongs to Chink and I, so I can really care less how anyone feels about my wanting to save them both," I said, getting emotional and angry.

"Dr. Wells, I'm Chasity's mother, and I would like for you to do what you need to do to make sure that she makes it out of surgery alive," Karen said.

"You're her mother of a good two weeks if that long. You have no fucking say," I yelled at her.

We all starting arguing back and forth about what decision should be made until the doctor heard enough. He told us that if we weren't able to agree on what decision was to be made, he would proceed as he saw fit.

"That's my friend in there, and I respect everyone's opinion, but she's all that I've got, and I would not want to live if something happened to her. Chink would want to live, and she would also want her unborn child to live. So with that being said, Doctor, you go back into that operating room and do what you feel is best, and if it comes to the decision of saving Chink or her unborn child, you save Chink," Polo cried.

I had forgotten that Polo was even in the room because she was so quiet until now. I respected what she said, and I understood it at the same time. I apologized to everyone in the room because I was being selfish out of fear of losing them both. I left the room to go out to get some air as the doctor left to get back to Chink.

LIEM

I left Polo to go and check on my brother, and I found him outside in front of the hospital. What I saw broke me down because I have always seen Lah as the strong one who's able to handle anything, but now, he looked broken.

"Hey bro, are you good?" I asked him.

"Yo, I don't claim to be a thug; I don't even claim to be tough, but on my unborn seed, that nigga is done. I know he did this shit to her, man. He couldn't be man enough to bring that shit to me, and for that, he will pay with his fucking life," he said with tears running down his face.

I walked over to him and pulled him into a brotherly hug, I really wished that I could stop the pain that he was feeling. I know it had a lot to do with the guilt of killing her mom and now her being laid up in the hospital, not knowing if she was going to make it or not - all because of his beef with Drone.

"Bro, I know this is hard, and it hurts like hell, but I promise you that we will get this nigga. But for right now, I need you to pull it together and be strong. Chink will survive this; she's a fighter, and you know it."

He let out a small smile; I really hated to see him in this state. He has always been there for me, and I'm going to be there for him even if that meant that I had to body Drone without him. He was too emotional right now to go at Drone. When we got back to the room, Karen looked upset. I know that Lah's words hurt her, but I hope that she understood that he didn't mean it and that he was acting off emotions at the thought of losing Chink and his unborn baby. The room door opened, and everyone looked up, thinking it was the doctor, but two detectives walked into the room. They asked a few questions and left their card with her aunt to call them when Chink was able to give a statement.

It was two hours later when the doctor reentered the room; he took a seat at the table. The room was so quiet that you could hear a pin drop.

"I have good news, and I also have some not so good news. The good news is that we were able to remove the bullet without causing any harm to the fetus."

"Thank you, Jesus," her aunt praised.

I looked over to Lah whose face showed no expression as he waited for the doctor to continue with the not so good news.

"Chasity suffered two seizures during surgery that leave us with some concerns. She's in recovery right now and will be there for the next hour. The next twenty-four hours are crucial, so we want to place her into the ICU where she will be monitored. The next twenty-four hours will help us determine if she will make a full recovery," he said.

The bad news wasn't good, but it wasn't that bad either. Like I said earlier, Chink is a fighter, and I have faith that she will pull through this.

"Are there any questions for me before I get back to my patients?" the doctor asked.

"When can we see her?" her uncle asked him.

"Once she is out of recovery, immediate family can visit two at a time with each visitor staying no longer than ten minutes," he answered.

Once the doctor left the room, Chink's aunt asked that everyone stand and hold hands as she led us into prayer.

"Father God, we come to you in the name of Jesus Christ. We believe all that you have promised, and we are here to claim it in Jesus' name. Lord, we believe that you've created this world by your word, and we believe that the word has power, and we are here to acknowledge it right now. As your word says, 'by his stripes, we are healed.' I command healing in Jesus' name. Let your word be accomplished right now. In the name of Jesus, we pray. Amen!"

We all responded with a resounding, "Amen!" as we all sat back down. Chink's aunt sat around telling stories of Chink as a child as she laughed and she cried. She uplifted the room and had everyone feeling a sense of calm that made the hour go by very fast. Everyone had their turn to visit Chink's room, and it was now time for Lah to go in to see her. I reminded him to be strong for her before he walked through the double doors.

CHAPTER TWENTY-ONE

LAH

I took a deep breath; I was scared to death to walk into her room because everyone that came out of the room said that she was awake. I didn't know what I was going to say to her. I didn't know if she was still mad at me, so I didn't know if I should go in and apologize or not mention it until she was better and out of the hospital. I walked into the room, and all the nervousness left my body as she smiled up at me. I stood over her, grabbed her hand, and the tears fell. I have never been in love before, and this was a new feeling for me. I kissed her hand and mumbled sorry as I let my other hand rub her stomach. I kept my hand on her stomach for a few minutes, saying a silent prayer of my own. I thanked the man above for getting her and my unborn baby through the surgery.

My ten minutes were ending, so I kissed her on the lips. I whispered in her ear that I loved her and that I would see her tomorrow. I walked out of the room angrier than I was before seeing her. I wanted Drone dead, before she left the hospital, because I will not give him another chance to hurt her again or to finish what he started.

Polo was saying her goodbyes to Chink's family when I walked out, so that gave me a chance to holler at Liem. I told him that we needed to do this and get it done before Chink was released from the hospital, and he agreed. I wasn't worried about him coming up to the hospital to finish the job because being that she was in ICU, she was on around the clock watch.

Liem, True, Jay, and I sat a block away from Drone's home. I had to recruit a few men because now that his punk ass knew that I was coming for him, he has about six dudes posted up inside with him. I made sure that everyone had a silencer attached so that we didn't disturb the neighborhood. True hooked up with the chick that lives directly across the street from Drone, so that's how we knew that he was home and how many dudes were in the house. I really didn't like to involve too many witnesses, but Liem vouched for these dudes.

I was planning on the element of surprise. Jay was a big ass dude that stood at six feet three and weighing about three hundred pounds. The plan was for the chick across the street to knock on the door. While they focused on who's at the front door, Jay will be kicking the back door in. The plan was for us to go in blasting everything moving. I drove a block over and parked while True called

216

up the chick and told her to wait ten minutes and then go across the street and knock on the door.

We all got out of the car and cut through the yard that would lead us directly to his back door. It was dark, and we were wearing all black, so I wasn't worried about anyone seeing us. I hope this chick was knocking on the door, because I just gave Jay the nod to knock the door off the hinges. Drone's ass claimed to have so much money, but he was living in this cheap ass house with no real security.

The element of surprise worked because those niggas didn't have time to retaliate as we bodied them, one by one. Drone wasn't among the dead, so Liem and I ascended the stairs, going from room to room, looking for his ass. He must have been hiding; I knew that his ass didn't hear the shots, but he had to hear that bitch screaming and the movement of the bodies dropping. I opened the last door at the end of the hall, and that nigga wasn't hiding. He was in here listening to some fucking music while his bitch was on her fucking knees, sucking him off. I had to control the urge of throwing up right there on the fucking floor. I wasn't here to play any games, and I damn sure wasn't waiting for the nigga to bust a nut as I walked up to her and shot her in the back of the head. His eyes were closed, but they opened as soon as her mouth let go of his little fucking baby penis. He instantly started bitching up upon seeing us.

"Yo man, it's not that fucking serious. We can squash this bullshit," he said.

"So shooting my girl and leaving her for dead isn't fucking serious?" I asked, busting him upside his fucking head with the gun.

His ass must have thought he killed her because his facial expression was priceless. It was also a dead giveaway that he was the perp. I didn't ask Chink who shot her because there was no need; I knew it was his ass.

"Come on man, we can still squash this bullshit. I shot your girl, but she lived, so that shit is water under the fucking bridge. You just killed my fucking girl, and I'm still willing to squash this shit," his bitch ass said.

"I killed your bitch because she put herself in something that didn't have shit to do with her ass. That fucking bullet had her name on it."

"Look man, you need to take this shit up with Karen. She's the reason that I was at the shop that night. I wasn't trying to kill your girl, man."

I swear this nigga is a bitch. Instead of taking his bullet like a fucking man, he wanted to go out being a snitch ass nigga. And as much as I hate a fucking snitch, I hate a fucking snake more, so I decided to hear his bitch ass out.

"Yo, pop this nigga so that we can get out of here," Liem said.

"Hold up, bro. Let this nigga talk. We're good. There were no gunshots heard, so there's no reason for the authorities to be called," I said.

"Speak nigga, and it better be worth my time." I gave his bitch ass a chance to speak.

Shit, if he wanted to use the time that he should be using to ask God for forgiveness before he meet his demise, who am I to stop him? I had to be honest when I say that I wasn't prepared for what had just come out of his mouth. Liem and I exchanged looks before I put a single gunshot wound between Drone's eyes. Before we headed out, I spit on his punk ass.

I had one more thing to take care of before leaving. After I grabbed the duffle bag out of the closet, we headed downstairs. I walked over to ole girl and popped her in the head because True's ass was over there consoling the bitch when he should have had the bitch dead already. I felt bad, but with no witnesses, I knew that I didn't have to worry about shit coming back to any of us because we all wore gloves. Unfortunately for her, the bitch saw our faces, so she had to go.

I dropped everyone off and was now sitting out front of my house in deep thought. I was trying to figure out what I wanted to do about the information that Drone just provided me with. I don't think I have another kill in me; this shit was becoming overwhelming.

CHAPTER TWENTY-TWO
CHINK

I couldn't thank God enough for sparing my life and my baby's life. I knew I was pregnant a week before getting shot. I was planning a special night to tell everyone together, but Cyn destroyed those plans. I knew that I didn't have to tell Lah who did this to me; I also knew that he would handle it, but I didn't think it would lead to a massacre. The news reported that this was one of the worst crimes committed in years. They still had no leads or any suspects at this time, and the case was an ongoing investigation. I just hope that shit doesn't come back to Lah. The detectives that visited when I was in the ICU came back to question me. I told them that I didn't know who the guy was; I told them that all I remembered was him asking me for the safe, and when I told him that I didn't have one, he shot me. I don't know if they believed me, but that was my story, and I was sticking to it.

"Hey, baby mama," Polo's crazy ass said, walking into the room.

"Polo, your ass is crazy," I laughed.

"I'm not crazy. I know if you scare me again, I'm going to kill your ass myself," she said.

"Shit, I didn't know that nigga was going to come for me, let alone shoot me. I heard about your crying ass," I laughed.

"Damn right. You're my sister, and I was scared to death that I was going to lose you. Don't you know that I love your ass and would die if something happened to you?" she said, tearing up.

I wiped and even fanned at my eyes, but the tears poured from my eyes like a waterfall, causing Polo to start crying too. It's a good thing that I was in a private room because we were bawling like two big-ass babies. I love my sister, till death do us part.

"If my eyelashes come off, I'm going to kick your ass, bitch," she laughed through her tears.

"I told you your ass is crazy. Weren't you just crying?" I laughed too.

"I can't believe I'm about to be a god mommy and an auntie," she said.

"I can't believe I'm about to be a mommy; I'm excited and nervous at the same time," I said seriously.

"You're going to be a great mother, and we are going to be great together. We're a team," she said.

"Come on, Polo. Stop making me cry. I think you get off seeing me cry," I said, pushing her.

"Nah, I'm just being real with you. I almost lost you, and I couldn't remember if I told you that I loved you. It was killing me, so every chance I get, I'm going to tell you how I feel," she smiled.

"Same here, and just so you know, you don't have to tell me because you show me. Now enough of these tear jerker conversations," I laughed.

"I'm about to bust this food down," she said, picking up the plate that my aunt cooked for me.

"Go ahead. I told my aunt that I was on a liquid diet for the next few days, but she brought it anyway, teasing my ass."

"Do you remember that time you lied to Mama Rita about having to stay after school so that we could go to the junior basketball game so that you could drool over Matt from Ms. Hanson's class? But it backfired because she came to pick you up and found out that you lied. She beat your ass and my ass." We laughed.

"I remember, and she didn't care whose child you were. She always said a liar deserves a sore ass; that was the same day her and your mom became good friends," I said, trying not to tear up again.

"Okay, Polo. We need to watch some television or something because you've got a bitch's chest hurting from laughing and eyes red from crying."

"Laughter and tears are good for the soul. Anyway, when are they letting you go home?"

"I have about another week or so before I'm cleared to go home. I just hope that my place is just the way I like it when I get home," I said.

"I don't know about all that, but it's still standing," she laughed.

"How are things going with you and your mom?" I asked.

"After you got shot, whatever happened between us didn't matter anymore. I needed my mom," she said, tearing up.

"Polo, I'm serious. You need to take your ass home," I said, laughing and wiping my eyes.

"I'm sorry. No more crying or joking," she said.

"So, how are things going with you and Lah?" she asked.

"We're good for the most part. I didn't get the chance to talk to him, but before this happened, I was going to tell him that I believed him."

"Well, for what it's worth, I believe him too," she said.

"Speak of the devil," Polo said as Lah and Liem walked into the room. Liem hugged me and released me, but when Lah hugged me, he didn't want to let me go. He kissed me on my lips, finally releasing me.

"How you feeling, Ma?" he asked me.

"I'm feeling much better. I'm just ready to go home and sleep in my own bed," I answered.

"How's the baby doing?"

"The baby is doing well; I started the prenatal vitamins today, and I'll be the first to say they taste like shit."

"And you tasted shit before?" Polo asked, laughing.

"Polo, what did I say about the jokes?" I laughed.

Polo and Liem looked so cute together. She was sitting in his lap, and he was whispering in her ear, making her smile. I'm happy for my girl, and I'm glad they were able to work it out because I believe he is the best thing that has ever happened to her. I laughed at how her mother was into young men, and Polo was the opposite and into the older men. She finally has someone who is in her age range, and the relationship couldn't be better. We played cards and joked around until it was time for visiting hours to end. Karen called to say that she wasn't able to make it up today, but she would be up tomorrow. Lah kissed me goodnight and told me that him and his mom were coming to visit me tomorrow - her request. I really didn't want her to come to the hospital to see me like this, but he insisted that we get it over with now.

The nurse came in after they left to check my vitals and to give me my next dosage of the medicine that the doctor had me taking every six hours. I tried to watch some television, but the medication was kicking in and my eyes were getting heavy, so I turned off the television and closed my eyes, falling asleep.

CHAPTER TWENTY-THREE

KAREN

I didn't make it up to the hospital yesterday, but I told Chink that I would see her today. I have been on an emotional roller coaster at the thought of losing her again. I was feeling physically sick because of what I'd done, and the nightmares that haunted me weren't helping. I was going to be a grandmother soon, and I didn't want anything to interfere with me being a part of the baby's life. I wasn't able to be in my daughter's life, so it would hurt me all over again not to be able to be there for Chink and her baby. I stopped in the lobby to get coffee and my morning muffin, and as I was walking in, Lah was walking out.

"Good morning, Karen. If you have a few minutes, I need to speak with you for a second," he said.

"Sure, no problem. Just give me a few seconds to get my coffee and muffin," I said.

I still had about thirty minutes before I needed to clock in, so I didn't have a problem seeing what he wanted to talk to me about. 'I hope that everything is okay with Chink and the baby,' I thought as I walked over to join him.

"How are you, Lah?" I asked as I sat down.

"I'm good, Karen. Just a little confused," he said.

"About?" I asked.

"When I came to talk to you about trying to convince Chink to hear me out about what I was being accused of, you said that you believed me. Why?"

"I believed you because like I said, I have always known you to be respectful and a nice guy. I just didn't see you capable of killing anyone."

"You've ever heard the saying, don't judge a book by its cover?" he asked me.

"Yes, I've heard the saying, Lah, but what does that have to do with anything?"

"Karen, I'm really not one to beat around the bush, so I'm going to just get straight to the point. When I came to you that day, you already knew that I went to Chink's house to kill her mom. You also knew that I didn't complete the job because you did," he said, sipping his coffee.

"You sound real crazy right now, Lah, and I don't have any idea what you're talking about."

"Karen, don't fucking sit here and bullshit me. Did you finish the fucking job or not?"

228

"Lah, you need to lower your voice; in case you haven't noticed, we are at the workplace," I said, ignoring his question.

"I wouldn't have to raise my voice if you weren't trying to sit here and bullshit me right now."

"I'm not trying to bullshit you, Lah. When I was told by Chink that her co-worker told her that you killed her mother, I had no idea that it was true until you just sat here and told me. The day that Chink's mom was stabbed was the same day that I decided that I was going to make her pay for all that she put me through. If Rita had agreed to tell Chink everything and was apologetic, I would have spared her life. Instead, the bitch sat there and acted as if she did me a favor by taking my fucking daughter," I said, getting angry.

I needed to calm down because I was getting emotional all over again at the thought of her nonchalant attitude.

"Like I said, Lah, I didn't know that you were involved. When I got back to her house, Rita was on the floor in her bathroom, choking off her own blood. I even felt sorry for her and thought about helping her, but just as quickly as that thought came, it left as I thought about all the pain that she caused me. I don't know what it is that you want from me, but I promise you one thing - if you're here to tell me that you're going to tell Chick about this, you better believe that if I go down, you're going down too," I told him.

"Karen, don't fucking threaten me. If I wanted to expose you, you would have been exposed already. What I will say is that Chink doesn't deserve to be hurt again, so if you agree to keep your fucking mouth closed, I will do the same," he said.

I really felt bad about my part in this, but my actions are justified. It bothers me that I went to bat for Lah, and his ass was involved. I honestly believed that he had nothing to do with Rita being killed. Now, with Drone being killed, I knew that was all him, and as my motherly instincts kicked in, I really felt some kind of way about him being with my daughter. I agreed with him; we would keep this between us and take it to the grave.

As I stood up to get to work, I thought that I didn't want to cause Chink any more pain, but I didn't want Lah in her life or my grandchild's life because he's a murderer. I didn't ask him why he went there that day to kill Rita, but I did have an idea why, and if he's capable of killing someone that did nothing to him, who's to say that he wouldn't kill for nothing again? I will say that I didn't feel sorry for Rita because karma is a bitch, and it paid her a deserving visit.

CHAPTER TWENTY-FOUR
CHINK

I was finally being released from the hospital today. It was only six am, but I was up even though discharge wasn't until noon. I was so happy to be going home; I couldn't sleep, and after the visit with Lah's mom, I was up all night trying to figure her ass out, so me being up had a little to do with her too. I really didn't expect her to come to the hospital being judgmental, and I didn't expect her to criticize Lah the way she was criticizing him, as if she was trying to belittle him in front of me. If I had to wrap up her visit in a few words, I would have to say that it was very uncomfortable, and I didn't like her because she has snob written all over her. Lah pleaded with me with his eyes because I was two seconds form reading her ass.

She had the nerve to ask me if my baby belonged to her son because me getting shot seemed like a love crime involving an angry boyfriend. Lah intervened, telling her that she was being rude and disrespectful, but she brushed him off as if he didn't say anything. She said that she was just making an observation and asking questions that she knew her son didn't ask. Talk about being offended, I'm just glad that Polo wasn't here because Lah would have been picking his mother's teeth up off the floor. I wasn't mad at him because he put her in her place, and he apologized to me. It was just sad that my child would not have a relationship with her unless her attitude changed, and I doubt that it would.

Karen came by later that day, and I really enjoyed her visit. She made me feel good about becoming a mother, and I knew that she would be supportive. As long as I have Lah, Polo, Karen, and my aunts, I just know that I would be okay.

Lah got to the hospital at noon, just as I asked him to, because he knew that once those discharge papers were signed, I would be ready to go. He carried my balloons and the plant that my stylist, Dymond, brought with her when she came to visit me. My house was spotless, just the way I like it. Polo rushed me, hugging me as if she hadn't seen me every day at the hospital. I went straight to my room and lay on the bed; oh, how I missed my bed. Lah laughed at me as I buried my face into my pillows. He got on the bed and spooned with me while I enjoyed the moment. I closed my eyes, enjoying being in his arms again.

"Um, excuse me, but didn't the doctor say no strenuous activity until he clears you at your next visit?" Polo asked, holding my discharge papers in her hand.

"Come on, Polo. Don't rain on my parade. I haven't got to spoon with my girl for almost a month," Lah laughed.

"I'm not worried about you two spooning; I'm worried about what that spooning is going to lead to," she joked.

"Yeah, whatever you say, sis. I'm about to head out and meet up with Liem," he said, getting up.

"Aww, I just got home, and you're leaving already," I whined.

"I'm not going to be long, bae. I just have some business to discuss with Liem," he said, kissing me.

"Okay, but the next time that you and Liem take off of work for me, it better be spent with me," I said.

"Don't worry; we'll be back in no time. Do you need me to bring anything back with me?" he asked.

"Nah, I'm good. I will see you when you guys get back. I want to shower and get comfortable in my own pajamas," I said.

After Lah left, I got my things that I needed to take a hot shower. Polo went back downstairs to wait on me to join her. I couldn't wait to tell her how Lah's mother showed her ass at the hospital.

I didn't let anyone know that I was having nightmares about the whole Drone situation. Even though I disliked him for what he had done to me, I kind of felt bad that him and Cyn had to lose their lives behind it. I know I shouldn't feel bad, because he could have killed me, but I guess it's the God in me.

LAH

I pulled up to Liem's apartment building, and it never fails, these niggas were always posted up. Liem let me in, and we headed to the back so that we could take care of business. Mama D was at work, and Cari was at school, so that was a good thing. No interruptions.

"What's up, bro?" I asked him.

"Just chilling," he said as he grabbed the gym bag out of the closet.

"I called True and Jay to meet us here like an hour ago, and neither one of them have hit me back yet," he said.

The night that we handled that shit with Drone, I noticed that True was acting real salty about my killing that bitch; he looked like he wanted to do something, so I had to dead that nigga. He and Jay were sitting in his car when I popped both those niggas. Now I had to let my bro know that they wouldn't be joining us at this meeting to get their split of this money. I know that I said that I didn't have another kill in me, but that shit came natural to me; I didn't even hesitate pulling the trigger. I haven't seen anything on the news about the murder, and I'm assuming Liem didn't either because he was waiting on those niggas to show up.

"Bro, True and Jay will not be joining us for this meeting," I said.

"You spoke to them?" he asked as he started removing the money from the bag.

"Nah, bro. I had to put those niggas to sleep," I said, deciding not to bullshit him.

"Why the fuck would you do some shit like that to my niggas? They helped us take Drone and his fucking men out for your ass!" he barked.

"Yo, calm your ass down. That bitch ass nigga, True, was salty about me taking that bitch out, so that tells me he didn't just meet that bitch. Jay got popped because when we walked up in there busting our guns, his gun didn't pop. His big ass was scared, and you know what they say about a scared nigga. So, both those niggas needed to be dealt with."

"Damn, I didn't peep none of that shit. I was just trying to get up out of there," he said.

"Bro, you should always observe and pay attention to what's going on around you. When I told you to hold the bag that night, those niggas were tight."

Those same niggas be out here claiming to be gangsta, but in reality, their asses are nothing more than a bunch of fucking punks.

"Good looking, bro," he said.

"What's the count?" I asked him.

"I counted that shit the same night I got here; it's a 100Gs. I split it up four ways, but now, I guess you and I have 50Gs apiece," he smiled, rubbing his hands together.

"Damn, that nigga had 100Gs at the crib where he laid his head at with niggas walking through that shit. I told you these fucking fake gangstas be doing the most, but his fuck up is my come up, so I'm not complaining," I said.

"Shit, you won't be hearing no complaining over here either. I just want to be smart with the money and get my Mom and Cari up out of these fucking projects. I know it's not a lot, but it's a lot for a down payment on something," he said.

"That's what's up, but I need for you to wait at least a month before making any moves so that shit don't seem suspect."

"I feel you bro, so I'm going to put my share of the money back into the bag, and you hold it because I don't want my ass to get tempted and go out here and splurge on nonsense."

"Cool, I'm going to head out and drop this money at the crib, and I will see you when I get to Chink's crib."

I pulled up to my house and noticed Mom's car was in the driveway; I didn't know why she was home and not at work. I'm glad that I have a separate entrance because I really didn't want to see her or talk to her. I have been giving her the cold shoulder for how she treated Chink at the hospital after she promised me that she would be cordial. I never introduced my mother to any female that I've ever dated, so she had to know that Chink was special. For her to insinuate that Chink's baby might have belonged to someone else really pissed me off. Instead of her being happy about being a grandmother, she was in there acting like a jealous fucking girlfriend. She apologized to me, but there was no sincerity behind it, so she's getting the cold shoulder until she shows me that she's really sorry and offers to apologize to Chink.

I opened the closet that I kept my safe in, put the money inside, and locked it back. I sat at my mini bar to have a drink before heading out. I had a lot on the brain - all the murders that I had under my belt and now I had to make a decision about whether or not I needed to add just one more. I didn't know if I could trust Karen to keep her fucking mouth shut about my involvement. Some people let guilt break them down and feel that they have to come clean, so if she was that type and felt like she needed to tell Chink and ask for her forgiveness, I didn't want her to implicate me. I also wanted to talk to Chink about moving out of that house, but I knew that it would be hard convincing her to move. When I first started seeing her and I asked her why she didn't sell the house, she said that if she moved and her mother decided to pay her a visit, she wouldn't know where to find her. It sounded crazy and I understood where she was coming from, but she has to keep in mind that she's about to have a child of her own, and the house is rather small to be trying to raise a family. I downed my drink and headed back out, en route to see my girl.

CHAPTER TWENTY-FIVE
CHINK

Lah and I were leaving my pre-natal appointment, and he was gloating, looking like he was walking on air. We were just told that we were having a boy, and his ass was hyped. I was a little disappointed because I wanted a little girl, but as long as my baby is healthy, I'm happy. I was almost seven months pregnant; it took us this long to find out the sex because we both agreed that we didn't want to know, but we both caved this time and wanted to know. We were on our way to Ruth's Chris Steak House, something we did every time we left my doctor's appointment. I have to say that I was happy with life right now. When my mother passed away, it was as if I couldn't get out of my funk until Lah came along. It wasn't a smooth ride, but I was definitely glad that I got on.

We walked into Ruth's Chris, and when Lah walked me into the seating area, I saw a few of my friends from the salon and my family. I thought that this was my surprise baby shower, but when Lah got down on one knee, the tears fell. I couldn't believe that he did this; I wasn't even dressed for the occasion. He knew that if his ass took me anywhere else on any other day, I would have known that something was up. I have been suspicious anytime he wanted to go out or go to visit someone. They said that I was making it hard for them to plan my shower, but I expressed to them that I didn't want a surprise shower; I wanted to be a part of it. I guess he fixed my ass. As I said, we always showed up here after my appointment because I always craved their stuffed chicken breast.

"Chasity Montgomery, we have been through so many ups and downs because the devil has been working overtime. I have to be honest with you; I have never been in love before - you are the first woman that I have ever loved. I'm no good at making a speech, so I need everyone to bear with me as I speak from my heart. I've never felt anything like this before; I go to sleep thinking about you, I wake up thinking about you, and I have come to the conclusion that I want this feeling to last forever. I want to go to sleep next to you every night, and I want to wake up to you every morning. Chink, will you marry me?" he asked me.

He pulled out the most beautiful ring that I've ever seen; I haven't seen many, but this was the best by far. The ring was set in diamonds that accentuated a round, brilliant center stone. The ring looked to be about two to three carats. I'm no expert, but the ring looked very expensive. It had my attention, and I almost forgot that Lah was still on his knee, waiting for my answer.

"Yes, I will marry you, Lahmiek Morales," I said, wiping my tears.

Everyone stood up and were now clapping and yelling congrats. Polo walked over to me with tears in her eyes, hugging me and telling me how happy she was for me.

"How does it feel that we got your snooping ass?" she asked me, laughing.

"I wouldn't say that I be snooping. I just want to be involved with my baby shower, but I didn't see this coming," I said.

I looked around the dimly lit restaurant, and when I noticed that Karen wasn't in attendance, I felt some kind of way. I pulled Polo to the side and asked her where Karen was. She said that they invited her, and maybe she was running late. Lah's mom and stepdad were even in attendance. His mom has tried to be cordial, and we've been getting along for the most part. We were all now sitting down eating, and as much as I was craving my stuffed chicken breast, I couldn't enjoy it because I was very upset that Karen still hasn't showed up. Lah stood up and hit his spoon against the glass, letting everyone know that he had an announcement to make.

"I just want to say thank you to everyone who took the time to come out. I know that some of you had to take off of work or even miss school today, and for that, I'm thankful. I had to plan it this way because my wife-to-be is always snooping, and we wouldn't have been able to pull this off if I'd tried for a later time or another venue. So again, thank you. As you all know, we came straight from our doctor's appointment, and I want you all to be the first to know that we are having a boy."

Everybody begun clapping again as the proud daddy-to-be took a seat. I didn't want Lah to know that something was bothering me, and if I didn't touch my stuffed chicken breast, he was going to know that I was upset. I didn't want to spoil what he put together. It was time to say our goodbyes and thank you's to everyone, letting them know that they would be on the guest list for our baby shower as well as our wedding. Once we got into the car, Lah asked me what was bothering me; I swear he knew me better than I knew myself. I thought that I did a good job of pretending that nothing was bothering me.

"I'm just a little upset that Karen didn't show up. I don't have my mom that raised me here, so I thought that she would at least have attended. Your mom doesn't even like me, and she showed up to support you," I said, tears falling.

"Babe, maybe something came up to where she couldn't be here," he said, making excuses for her.

"What's more important than being here for her daughter's engagement luncheon?" I asked him.

"Do you want to stop by her house to see if everything is okay because I believe that she would have called if she wasn't going to be able to make it?" he asked.

"Yes, let's stop by, and if she's there, she better have a good reason as to why she didn't show up."

We pulled up to her house, and Lah helped me out of the car. This stomach was beginning to interfere with me getting up once I sat down. Lah knocked on the door, and we waited, but she didn't answer. I pulled out my phone to call her, and as the phone rang, it could be heard inside of the door. I went into my bag to retrieve the key that I had to her place, and we went inside. She wasn't downstairs, so I got my big belly ready to climb the stairs to see if she was in her room, sleeping. When I walked into the foyer, it was like déjà vu as I saw her lying on the floor near the living room table. I screamed, and Lah came running behind me. I was numb; I heard him calling 911, but I couldn't move. I stood in the middle of the floor crying; I didn't understand what was going on. It looked like she took her own life because the gun was still in her hand. Lah grabbed my hand and walked me toward the kitchen. He left me seated at the table while he went to let EMS and the police officers in.

'I went from having two mothers to having no mother at all,' I thought as my body heaved up and down. Lah did everything that he could think of to calm me down, because of the baby, but I couldn't help it. He called Liem and told him to get Polo to Karen's house because I needed her. He wanted me to leave, but I told him that I wasn't leaving. I started to hyperventilate which wasn't good for the baby at all. The paramedics told me that I needed to try to calm down for the baby, or they were going to have to give me a sedative. Polo walked in, and I cried in her arms as she rubbed my back, telling me that I needed to calm down. EMS took my vitals - just to make sure that I was okay.

"Polo, why would she do this?" I asked, just above a whisper.

"Shush, just try to calm down," she said, continuing to rub my back.

Lah has started to worry about me. Since Karen's death, I have been very depressed. I tried to get out of the funk that I was in, but I just couldn't find the strength. Everything was put on hold; we were supposed to be in our new home before the baby was born, but that has been put on the back burner. My baby shower was canceled because I just didn't feel like being around anyone right now. I was already two weeks overdue, and the doctor believes it has to do with stress.

Lah, Polo, Liem, and I were on our way to the hospital; my doctor was inducing my labor today. I'm not going to lie, I was excited about meeting my little man; I think this was my first time smiling since Karen's death. Polo was more excited than I was; the baby wasn't even here yet, and she was talking non-stop about what he was going to wear home.

I was in labor for eight hours and twenty-three minutes; the pain was unbearable at times, but when I looked at my little man for the first time, I didn't even remember the pain. Lahmiek Terrell Morales, Jr. was seven pounds, eight ounces. He was handsome, the splitting image of his father, who was beaming as he and Polo argued about who was going to hold him next. I laughed at both of them for being so silly. Lahmiek Jr.

was late, but he was right on time; my spirits were lifted as soon as he was placed in my arms.

I was released from the hospital today, and I couldn't wait to get home with my new baby and my husband-to-be. He stood by me through my whole depression stage, and I loved him for that. I was going to try to move on and be the best mother and wife that I could be. Although I miss Karen and my mom, I know that they are always going to be a part of me and will always watch over me. I smiled getting in the car, excited about starting the next chapter in my life.

EPILOGUE

Lah was upstairs with the baby, and I was in the kitchen making dinner; being a new mom has been the blessing that I needed to get over my depression stage. After Karen's funeral, I really didn't want to go on anymore; my son was a blessing sent from above. Lahmiek Jr. is such a good baby, and he keeps a smile on my face.

Just as I was about to put my macaroni and cheese into the oven, the doorbell rang. Whoever was ringing the doorbell continuously was acting as if they lost their damn mind. At first, I thought that it was Polo because she sometimes rings the bell like she's crazy, but when whoever it was started banging on the door, I knew that it wasn't her. I opened the door and there were six officers gracing my doorstep.

"Hello, how can I help you?" I asked, with my voice cracking.

My heart felt as someone was playing the drums on it with the way it was beating inside my chest. I swear that I didn't need any more bad news because I wouldn't be able to handle it. My nerves were past being on edge; they'd jumped off the cliff.

"Ma'am, we have an arrest warrant for Lahmiek Morales for the murder of …"

To Be Continued...

CPSIA information can be obtained
at www.ICGtesting.com
Printed in the USA
LVOW10s1449090817

544393LV00014B/773/P